KU-576-956

RIVER OF GOLD

FAY GOLDIE

RIVER OF GOLD

Illustrated by William Papas

London
OXFORD UNIVERSITY PRESS
1969

Oxford University Press, Ely House, London W. 1

GLASGOW NEW YORK TORONTO MELBOURNE WELLINGTON
CAPE TOWN SALISBURY IBADAN NAIROBI LUSAKA ADDIS ABABA
BOMBAY CALCUTTA MADRAS KARACHI LAHORE DACCA
KUALA LUMPUR SINGAPORE HONG KONG TOKYO

First published 1969

For Meg and Peta,
with whom I fossicked
at Mac Mac and at
Pilgrim's Rest, and
found great treasure.

PRINTED IN GREAT BRITAIN BY
WESTERN PRINTING SERVICES LTD., BRISTOL

CONTENTS

I

Kangaroo Joe

If he hadn't been tightly wedged between Kangaroo Joe and the Hottentot, Hendrik, who cared for the mules, Tom might well have been catapulted from his precarious perch on the driver's seat of the postcart as it swung round a bend.

The mules seemed to have sensed that they were nearing the end of their journey, and their hoofs drummed out an exciting tattoo. Dust rose in smothering clouds and drifted across the winter-dry veld in the wake of the lurching, bumping, over-laden cart, a light wind from the south dispersing it.

The road they travelled was no more than a wide track beaten across the veld and over the hills by wagons and horsemen, the boots and home-made velskoen of tramping adventurers in their endless search for diamonds and gold, and the leather-hard soles of the feet of jog-trotting brown men.

'There she lies—there's Pretoria!' Kangaroo Joe shouted, and pointed ahead with his whip.

Tom Maxwell knuckled his burning eyes and peered through the dust and glare.

At first he could not make out anything beyond the familiar stunted thorn-trees and vast undulations of veld, with the wagon trail unrolling ahead of them in the shimmering haze.

Then, suddenly, his eyes picked up the gleam of whitewashed walls as the late afternoon sun struck them, and the dark smudges of trees. The pattern of the little town slowly became clearer.

If this was journey's end Tom knew it was also the start of the great adventure that had filled his mind through the long months of travel by sea and land, since leaving the farm on the outskirts of North London that had been his home. He had remained in England after the death of his parents, for his father's cousin had taken the farm over, and had welcomed Tom into his family.

During the past year letters had arrived from his Uncle Andrew

and a few from Aunt Polly, with an occasional scrawled note from his cousin Samantha, who had always been like a sister to him. The family had emigrated to South Africa shortly before Tom's parents had died, and his uncle had written at once on hearing the sad news, promising to send for Tom to join them if they decided to settle in that far land.

From their letters Tom had built pictures in his mind of the capital of the Transvaal, or United Republic, as they sometimes referred to it. He had assumed that Pretoria would be a city. Of course, not as vast as London, but certainly large in size and importance. 'Capital' was an impressive word.

Now disbelief replaced Tom's first excitement at Kangaroo Joe's shout. Could that small village really be Pretoria? Surely not. Why, it was no more than a sprawl of cottages in a wide valley, made even more insignificant by the hills that surrounded it.

Tom grabbed his companion's arm. It felt as hard as iron, the muscles taut as the man controlled his mule team.

'You mean,' Tom yelled above the rattle and creak, and the thudding hoof-beats, 'you mean—that hamlet's Pretoria?'

The big man grinned down at him through the wild bush of his whiskers.

'Yeh, m'lad. That's Pretoria right enough. Don't impress you, eh? Waal, let me say it don't impress me neither. Why should it now? It's jest a place where it suits some folks to build their shacks —together like. Ain't nothing impressive about that. Plain foolish if you ask me, with all this land going begging. You want yer eyes to pop, Tom? Wait till you get to the diggings, lad. That's something that'll really knock you.'

'But they call this a capital.'

'Suits them to give it a fancy name. Don't mean a go-darn thing. Jest their way of saying President Burgers most times lives here, if he ain't on his farm or at Potchefstroom, and a man called Paul Kruger. An' the British Red Coats have their camp here. You'll see 'em strut around like turkey-cocks, Tommy boy.'

'My uncle thinks Paul Kruger is a great man. He's often mentioned him in his letters. Do you think I'll be able to see President Burgers and Paul Kruger, Kangaroo?'

'Can't think what's to stop you seeing them. The President's a friendly tyke—a real digger's chum, out for our rights. Paul Kruger's a great darn mountain of a man. Preaches in the church, but mostly, seems to me, he jest sits and talks, world without end, Amen. Clever, though. Clever as a bagful of monkeys. But not clever enough to appreciate the colour of gold. Paul Kruger loves this land, Tom. We've gotta be fair, and I can see his point in a kinda way. He likes it the way he thinks God made it. Quiet and peaceful—'cept for fighting, which comes natural to man. White man against black man—black man against white or black man—white man against white man. Plenty of bloodshed, but all in the family, if you get what I'm driving at, Tom. Tidy.

'What makes him hopping mad is the way us diggers is swarming onto the scene. Gold-mad, some of us tykes. We don't give a damn if it's Africa or Australia, New Zealand or any place else. Jest so's the gold's here. We want that gold. Do we want it! And when we've got it, we'll push off. We'll only leave the holes we've dug to show we've ever been here, and nature'll soon fill those in with bush and grass. Paul Kruger calls us thieves. Maybe we are at that. But gold was planted in the earth for men to nose out and use. It's against nature to expect us to leave it there for ever. Don't make sense—not to us it don't.'

In the week they had spent together, Tom had grown very

close to the giant of a man who now sprawled on the seat beside him. In fact he felt closer to Kangaroo Joe than he had ever felt to anyone in his life.

He hadn't asked himself why this was so. But the digger was his friend. And he was also the personification of all the great adventurers Tom had ever read about, dreamt about, and in whose raw-hide boots he had dared to imagine himself—adventuring.

The way the Australian had come into Tom's life had been characteristic of the man.

Before the second stage had been reached on the long journey up from D'Urban, Jan Pretorius, the driver of the postcart, had been thrown from his seat when the cart struck a pot-hole. And it was while Tom and Hendrik, and the two passengers who travelled on the piled luggage and merchandise in the back of the cart, were gathered round the unconscious man, that Kangaroo Joe had come swinging up the hill behind them, swag on shoulders, battered ten-gallon hat pushed back on his head. He wore a red flannel shirt and moleskin trousers, thick-soled boots and a waistcoat made of springbok hide. Round his hips was a wide leather belt with a silver buckle—the finest belt Tom had ever seen.

'Fell off his perch, did he?' Kangaroo Joe asked, a twinkle in his eyes. With one deft movement he swung the load down from his shoulders and placed it at the side of the road. 'Takes all sorts to drive a postcart, I guess. Ah.' He jerked a bottle from the driver's pocket. 'Gone to the last drop, the son-of-a-gun.'

'He's a good driver,' Tom felt forced to say in defence. 'This is a badly sprung cart, mister, and it's overloaded. And this isn't a road at all. It's—it's—'

The newcomer had been bending over the driver, examining him with quick, expert hands for possible injuries. Now he threw back his head and studied Tom with his astonishingly bright blue eyes.

'Waal, one thing this road ain't,' he drawled. 'It *ain't* the road to hell. The Book tells us that's smooth an' downhill all the way. Don't worry, I wasn't taking a poke at this little feller. I've had a thirst mesself many's the time—and I've fallen good'n' heavy.'

And it was then, as his white whiskers parted and he smiled up at Tom, that the first bond was forged between them.

Kangaroo Joe picked the driver up in his arms as though he were a child, and placed him in the back of the cart.

'Nothing wrong with him that a bit of jolting won't put right,' he said calmly. 'You two get on up with him and watch out he don't roll off again.'

He heaved his truck up beside them, and climbed into the driver's seat.

From that moment on he took command, and nobody questioned him. Tom was to find that very seldom indeed did anyone ever question the big man, and when one did, the lesson learned was sharp and long remembered.

At Pietermaritzburg the driver was handed over for rest and repairs, and the postcart authorities were only too relieved to accept Kangaroo Joe's offer to substitute for him. The weekly mail-run from D'Urban to Pretoria had only recently been started, and drivers were hard to come by.

'I know mules like I know my own brothers,' Kangaroo Joe had said. 'And I've done this trail before. Anyway, Hendrik will keep us headin' in the right direction if I'm in doubt. He knows the run like his own game trail, I can see that.'

Apparently he had not been unknown in Pietermaritzburg, and his reputation was sound.

They had been driving up the north road the next day when Tom asked:

'Why are you called Kangaroo Joe?'

'Waal, you wouldn't know it yet, maybe, but all of us diggers get christened with names we've earned. Our mates see us different from how our ma's and pa's saw us when we was young 'uns. They called us Steve an' Charlie an' Bill an' Jack. But our buddies gave us the names that really grow out of us.

'Why d'you suppose I'm called Kang-groo Joe? It ain't jest because I come from down under where 'roos are mostly called Joeys. It's because I lope along kinda easy seeming, but fairly jumping the miles.

'This ain't no way for a man to travel, Tom, perched up here like a monkey on a box. Suits me right now because I'm in a kinda haste to get to the new diggings before all the claims is jumped.

But it ain't no way for a man to move around. Stiff and sore come nightfall, from bouncing about on this old wooden mailbag box we call a seat.

'Wait till you hoist your swag on your shoulders, grub-stake, blanket, billycan, pick-'n'-shovel, the whole bloomin' lot, and set your stride long and easy for the skyline. Jest yourself in all the world around you—jest you, and the gold you're out to get your hands on. Sometimes the thought of gold gets to be like a fever in your blood. But most times it's no more'n the fleas that keep this old dog awake and scratching—and moving on.'

As they travelled north Tom watched Kangaroo Joe's fine white whiskers turn the colour of the dust of the long road as it settled and stained them. Today brown, or red, or streaky grey. The bushy eyebrows that overhung the man's eyes were also coloured dust-traps. Only his thick thatch of hair was always white when Joe removed his hat at the end of the day, and dunked his head in the bucket of steaming water which Hendrik brought before the evening meal, together with soap and a grey cotton blanket.

After lathering then rinsing his head, beard and all, Kangaroo Joe would shake it as a dog shakes the water from its body after swimming a river. Then he would rub dry his mane of hair and his whiskers on the blanket, combing his hair down with his fingers before clapping his hat back on his head, and taking his place at the table.

Tom had listened, entranced, to the tales Kangaroo Joe told as they sprawled in the shade or round the camp fire during their midday breaks for food and rest; and while sitting close on the driver's seat during the long hours on the road.

Hendrik knew no English, so he would sit silently, staring ahead or dozing as they drove. Sometimes he would twang a jew's harp, held between his teeth, repeating the few notes of the tune over and over again.

It seemed to Tom now that a whole lifetime had been spent on that journey up from the coast. He would always remember the frost-crisp mornings, brilliant, burning days, and freezing nights when sleep came immediately he huddled in his blankets and closed his eyes.

They had put up at some strange places on their way, to eat, and sleep, and rest or change their mules. These recognized post-cart stages had been at farm homesteads, and wood and iron hotels in little towns. And once, when they had been forced to take shelter in a wayside trading store while a violent storm beat down on them, they had stretched out on the counter or hunched themselves restlessly on bags of grain. And they had been tormented all through the night by the wild scampering and squeaking of rats.

'Why do you shake and bang your boots when you take them off, Joe?' Tom had asked one night when the performance kept him awake.

'Now that's a go-darn silly question.' Kangaroo Joe's eyes had been round in mock surprise. 'To see there ain't no toes or golden sovereigns left behind in these old boots, to be sure.'

And their laughter had brought a protesting shout from the bedroom on the other side of the thin partition—'Shut up, can't you, and let honest folk sleep!'

The next morning, when the boots were again being violently slapped and shaken before they were pulled on and laced, Tom said in a stage whisper, 'Still looking for toes and sovereigns, Kangaroo Joe?'

This time the answer was serious.

'Every digger empties out his boots before pulling them on, Tom. You remember to do the same, lad. Scorpions, spiders, and them deadly little night adders often crawl into boots at night, looking for some place warm and dry. Many a one I've caught this way when dossing down in the veld or under canvas.'

The big man's preparations for the night had surprised Tom as much as his own long flannel night-shirt had amused the digger.

'Haven't seen one of them fancy duds but once before in my life,' Kangaroo Joe commented dryly, laughter in his eyes. 'Mighty dangerous and draughty by the looks of them.'

He certainly took no chances with draughts. His hat was pulled down more firmly at night, his belt unbuckled, and waistcoat and trousers unbuttoned. After the ritual of removing his boots they were carefully placed close to hand.

'Always have your boots in smellin' distance, Tom,' he had warned. 'Thieves go for 'em next to gold. Tramping in a country like this, where'd a man be without his boots? Take no chances,

boy. Remember my words of experience. Boots are a man's best friend.'

More buildings were emerging from the trees as the postcart approached Pretoria. But it was still no more than a hamlet.

Tom stared ahead with interest. After all, nothing had been as he had imagined it would be on this journey. And, if the towns of D'Urban and Pietermaritzburg had been much smaller than he had expected them to be, how much greater had been everything else in this new land—the veld and sky, the mountains and valleys.

He could not have imagined that there would be springbok in such vast herds that the earth shook with the thunder of their tiny hoofs as they passed like great cloud-shadows across the veld. That he would see elephant, giraffe and a hippopotamus in the distance, and many kinds of large and small buck near at hand. That eagles would glide on such wide, still wings against the blue. Or that stars would shine so brightly in the night sky, like glittering diamonds scattered just out of reach.

A sudden thought made Tom turn to his friend. 'Kangaroo

Joe, what will you do when we get to Pretoria?' he asked, and his voice was anxious. Until then he had been living in each exciting moment of their journey, and had not given thought to what might lie ahead.

'What'll I do? I'll be on my way, Tom. And mighty glad to. I'll stretch my legs and be off.'

'But where will you go?'

'To the new diggings at Mac Mac to be sure. Where else?' The man's eyes shone. 'There're rumours of great strikes there, Tom. Great darned lumps of gold you can hardly lift from the river-bed. They say there's a river of gold—Say, now!' He broke off, pointing ahead. 'Who's that riding hell for leather to meet us? It don't look to me like the President, or yet Paul Kruger—'

'It's—yes, *it's Sammy*!' Tom shouted, and waved his hat in the air.

'Hey, steady there young feller. You'll be pitching out if you're not careful. Whar, now!' Kangaroo Joe pulled in the mules to a canter, a trot—to a halt. And the girl swung her horse alongside.

'Tom!' she cried. 'Oh, Tom, here you are! I thought you'd never get here. This is the third day I've ridden out to meet you.'

'Where did you learn to ride like that?'

'Here, of course, silly. There's a horse waiting for you, too. Oh, we can't talk here. Don't let's waste time. I'll race you into town. Come on!'

And Samantha was off like the wind, her laughter floating back as Kangaroo Joe flicked the mules to pursuit, and Tom hung on for his life.

2

Gold Rush Fever

Tom sometimes thought he had never in his life been as cold as he was during that winter of 1873 in Pretoria.

Even the water furrows on either side of each street, which provided crystal water to the four-hundred-odd inhabitants of the town, were often frozen in the morning, and the veld shone white with hoar-frost until the sun broke through the heavy ceiling of mist to thaw it.

His Uncle Andrew had insisted that Kangaroo Joe spend the night with them before setting out for the diggings, and Tom had been happily surprised to find how well the two men got on in spite of the fact that they were quite different in almost every way.

Their talk was all about gold and the chances of 'striking it rich'. They each had exciting stories to tell of men whom they knew, or had heard about, who had made fortunes overnight at Mac Mac in the Eastern Transvaal.

Samantha and Tom listened, spellbound, to the talk that went on all through the evening meal, and later, when they were gathered in front of the log fire in the living-room.

Only Aunt Polly remained untouched by the excitement of it. Her face had a closed, cold look, and she sat close to the ring of lamplight, stitching away at her mending as though she were in a sad little world by herself.

It was only when the talk turned to Tom's journey, and especially to their relatives and friends in England, that she showed interest, and then she would question Tom closely, as though hungry for news of the place she still called 'home'.

'It's a pity you can't come on down with me to the diggings, and have a dekko for yourself, Mr. Howes,' Kangaroo Joe said.

Tom knew that his friend much preferred his own company to

that of others when hitting the trail, and he realized what a real bond of friendship had been struck between the two men.

Andrew Howes glanced at his wife's bowed head.

'There is nothing I would like better than to come with you, my friend,' he said. 'But I am afraid it will have to wait awhile.'

'Take a tip from an old digger, mister. Don't put it off too long and miss yer chance. The Gold Rush is on. It's on *now*. I know what I'm talkin' about because I've been in on 'em before this. In my own country, in New Zealand and Canada. First-comers strike it lucky, an' those what tail along behind have to take what's left.'

Aunt Polly let her sewing fall to her lap. She looked directly at the big Australian, and her eyes were angry.

'You say you have taken part in other—Gold Rushes?'

'That I have, ma'am. Most all of 'em that's happened along in my time.'

'Then you must surely be a very rich man?'

Kangaroo Joe's laugh filled the room.

'It's easy come, easy go, ma'am. Us diggers don't hold onto our gold. Not most of us, anyways. There's those that know how to salt the yeller stuff away, and the rest of us think we'll know how to *next* time we strike it rich. But most of us never do learn.'

'That is what I thought.'

Kangaroo Joe studied her hostile face. He was no longer laughing. Tom thought he had never seen his friend look—kinder. It was almost as though he felt sorry for Aunt Polly.

'I reckon it's this way with us, ma'am,' he said slowly. The words did not come easily. 'With some of us—p'haps most of us —it's the fossicking after gold that's the game. It's everything a digger's life stands for—the, well call it the challenge, if you like. Being on your lonesome with nothing to depend on but y'own two hands and the eyes in y'head. It's being out there under the sky with a good pair of legs under you, and everything that's yours in the world—on your bloomin' back. It's waking every morning thinking *today's the day*. My lucky day! I'm going to strike the yeller stuff before the sun goes down. Y'can feel it in your bones some days.

'All right. So it's a trick this gold-fever plays on a man. You don't find a speck o' the stuff no matter what your bones told you. At the end of the day you've got nothing to show for your hard work. Only your achin' back and torn hands. Or p'haps jest a little gold to add to yer tin. But there's tomorrow, see? You don't know—nobody knows—what'll come along tomorrow. But you keep slogging away, you keep fossicking, you keep darn well hoping.

'What I'm trying to say is this, ma'am. Some folks is only happy if they strike it rich. Good an' rich. They don't want to be diggers. They want to be rich. They want the things gold can buy —not jest the yeller stuff itself.'

'But surely that is reasonable?'

'To those folks it is, I guess. But not to us others. We wouldn't want to live in a grand house with nothing to do but count our wealth. That's why lots of us throw the stuff away, living wild, or jest giving it away I guess, even when we find a load. I know. I've done it plenty. It's our freedom we want, ma'am. The open, tough life of the veld or the prairie. It's the excitement. It's—I guess it's jest the today an' tomorrow life that gets us. No yesterday. No day after tomorrow. Jest today an' tomorrow. I couldn't want it any other way mesself.'

The today and tomorrow life. Tom thought he knew what his friend meant. He had experienced a taste of that kind of life on their journey to Pretoria. And it had been the best thing he had ever known. Falling asleep at night dog-tired. Waking to a new day with a feeling of great excitement.

'To my mind,' Aunt Polly was saying stiffly, 'a digger's life is a kind of madness. You will forgive me for speaking so plainly.'

'No offence. It's the way you see it, ma'am. But, if you'll pardon me, ma'am, y've never known the kinda life I'm talking about, have you? Matching y'self up against nature. Living kinda wild.' He broke off, suddenly embarrassed, and smiled at Mrs. Howes. 'Sorry I've been rambling on. I'm grateful to you for all your kindness. Think I'll be turning in, if it's the same to you good folks. I'm hitting the road soon's I've laid in grub for the journey in the morning.'

'Oh, I didn't notice the time!' Mrs. Howes exclaimed. 'Samantha, Tom, to bed at once. You must be bone-tired, dear lad, after your long journey. How very thoughtless we have been.'

Candles, in copper candlesticks, were brought from the kitchen and handed round. And Mrs. Howes went from one to the other with a lighted taper. She was smiling and friendly now, almost the Aunt Polly whom Tom remembered from across the great gulf of a year ago. In the soft, flickering light, one didn't notice the little lines that drew her brows together, and turned down the corners of her mouth.

'Good night,' she said to Kangaroo Joe. 'May tomorrow be bright and clear for your journey.'

'Thank you, ma'am. And good night to you.'

It was a sound like a thunderclap that awoke Tom at first light the next morning. He started up in bed, his surroundings strange to him.

'Go-darn it!' came in a hoarse whisper from the other side of the room. And again there was that great explosion of sound.

Tom had never heard anyone sneeze like it.

'Oh, Kangaroo Joe!' He laughed in relief. 'I thought the world had been blown apart with a keg of gun-powder.'

'I knew it would happen when I left m'head unprotected,' Joe grumbled. 'First time in twenty years or more I've taken a meal without me hat on—an' slept without it, too! Asking for trouble. Draughts kill off more men than wild beasts or strong drink, Tom. Remember those words of experience.'

'Are you ill, Kangaroo Joe? Will you remain here—?'

'I wouldn't dare!' the digger cried, swinging his legs out of bed and reaching for his hat. 'It'd kill me quicker'n a flash of lightning, Tom. I'll be all right once I'm belting along on the trail. Sweat it out. That's the thing.' And again he nearly sneezed his head off.

Although the outer walls of the house were of unbaked brick, lime-washed, all the walls inside were of wood. So it was not only Tom who was rocketed out of his sleep by Kangaroo Joe's sneezing.

'I'll get the fire going and make some coffee, my dear,' Andrew Howes said, shivering as he wrapped himself in his red woollen dressing-gown. 'You stay where you are.'

He found Samantha in the kitchen, yawning, and breaking kindling as she carefully laid the fire in the huge black stove.

'The water has frozen in the bucket, Papa,' she said. 'Will you please break it up and fill the kettle.'

'Leave it to me and go back to bed, Samantha. There is no need for two of us to catch a chill by rising so early in the morning.'

'Two of us? You surely mean *three*, Papa! Poor Kangaroo Joe must have blown the top off his head, sneezing like that. He really has done the roosters out of their job this morning.'

When Mrs. Howes eventually joined her family in the warm kitchen, neat as a pin in her grey woollen dress and blue apron, she found them all still drinking coffee, hands wrapped around their enamel mugs. And their lively faces and excited talk proved that they had started up where they had left off the night before.

'Ah, Polly, come and get warm, my dear.' Her husband got up from his chair and invited her to take it. 'We were just talking about—'

'I can guess the subject. Gold! Do you realize that none of you is dressed—except our guest?'

'No credit to me, ma'am. I sleep this way,' Kangaroo Joe said smugly. 'Saves time and trouble and—*atisho*!—safeguards the health as well.'

Samantha laughed. 'How can we believe you? You are the only one who has a cold!'

'Samantha,' her mother said sternly, 'go to your room at once and dress.'

Sheepishly, and with all haste, her husband and Tom followed Samantha from the kitchen.

'It's this Gold Rush fever, ma'am,' Kangaroo Joe said gently.

'I sometimes think this country has gone quite mad. Gold Rush fever! It is all one ever hears. Respectable men we know have left their families, their farms and businesses, and—and gone off to dig for gold. Mr. Kruger is right. Gold is the ruination of this land. Would that he were President instead of Mr. Burgers, who champions the diggers and encourages them.'

'Have you all the wood you need, ma'am, or shall I chop some logs?'

'There is no need—'

'But I'd welcome it. My arms are aching from hanging idle. It would be a favour, ma'am.'

'The logs and axe are in the little shed in the garden. Thank you, Mr.—Mr. Joe.'

*

'Samantha and Tom are going over to Mitchell's to fetch the mule after breakfast,' Mr. Howes told his wife when they were all seated round the kitchen table, eating large bowls of porridge. There was the spicy smell of baking bread in the room, and a lamp burned on the Dutch cupboard. It was a cosy scene. 'Kangaroo Joe will make much better time to the diggings if his—his clobber is carried for him.'

'I'm used to humping my swag,' the digger interrupted.

'But the mule is a liability to me. You will do me a favour by taking it, I assure you. I exchanged the rest of the team for two horses after we had lost a mule to lions when they were out to graze on the commonage. We are plagued by lions that come into the valley of a night along with the game. This place has for long been a sanctuary for them, it seems, with its shelter, water and grazing. I have no stable, so a friend on the far side of the commonage allows my animals to share his barn with his mules and oxen.'

'Then I'll buy it from you. You're right, it'll save me time on the journey sure enough.'

'Accept it as a gift, friend. One seldom talks of selling one's possessions in Pretoria. There is no money here, as you know, or little of it. We barter with one another. And I am bartering my mule for the interest and entertainment you have already given us.'

Kangaroo Joe stretched across the table and shook his host's hand.

'One day I'll pay my part of the bargain,' he said.

'The mule is salted. That was why I was given the horses in exchange for some of my team. The horses, of course, aren't salted, and the man was on his way south into fever country—the Lowveld.'

'What do you mean by "salted", Uncle Andrew?'

'We mean animals that have recovered from sleeping-sickness, and are consequently immune to it. Tom. It's a terrible scourge, especially on the Lowveld during the hot months.'

When the meal was over, Samantha and Tom set off across the track of veld they called the commonage, while Kangaroo Joe went to wake up a storekeeper and buy all he would need for his journey.

The valley was smothered in mist through which the early sun was struggling to shine.

'Be careful that the grass doesn't cut you, Tom,' Samantha warned as they followed the winding footpath that had been worn through the waist-high grass. 'The frost can cut like a knife.' Her hands were buried in her pockets, and a knitted cap had been pulled down to protect her ears.

Twice grey shapes emerged from the mist which, to Tom's surprised delight, proved not to be cattle, but kudu.

'The buck and other wild creatures move away from the town when day breaks,' Samantha explained. 'These are the last of the stragglers. Sleepy-heads!'

The family gathered in the yard to watch Kangaroo Joe load the mule.

Mrs. Howes gave him a parting gift of two loaves hot from the oven and wrapped in a cloth, and she bade him a friendly farewell.

'May we accompany Kangaroo Joe just a little way, Mama?' Samantha begged.

'I need your help in the house, Samantha. But you may go if you turn back at the town boundary. Do not waste time.'

'Oh, thank you, Mama!'

'This is not farewell. We shall meet again, my friend,' Andrew Howes said as he shook the digger's hand.

'That I know. I will stake a claim for you beside my own.'

It was while the children were returning home after seeing their friend out of sight that Tom had the fright of his life.

They were hurrying down the road when an ant-hill attracted his attention. On the journey up from the coast he had often used one for a seat during a halt, or had climbed up onto a particularly high one to command a wider view.

The dome of hard-packed earth rose to about four feet from the grass that grew between the road and the water furrow, and Tom took a flying leap from a boulder and landed on top of the ant-hill.

Unfortunately the crust was thin and the ant-hill hollow, and with a shout of surprise Tom felt it give way under him.

Looking down, his heart froze in horror. Several snakes were writhing about his feet. As he tried to get a foothold on the broken edge of the ant-hill, so it crumbled away.

His shout brought Samantha running to him.

'Here—give me your hand—and jump for it!' she cried, gripping his hand and pulling with all her strength.

Fear did the rest, and Tom was soon safely on the road again, although badly shaken by his ordeal.

'It's the cold weather,' his cousin explained. 'Snakes often take refuge in ant-hills and under rocks in winter. Oh, Tom, what a good thing you were wearing boots!'

In his mind Tom heard Kangaroo Joe warn him, 'Remember, Tom, boots are a man's best friend.'

'It seems so strange, Sam, that here in the tropics it should be so cold. Even your snakes find it unnatural.'

'Oh, winter's not for very long,' his cousin tried to reassure him. 'This is the end of June. Next month it will be the beginning of spring with any luck. Winter came early this year. You can see the first buds coming out on the peach-trees and rose bushes already. I'll show you. That's one of the wonderful things about it here, Tom. One day it's winter, and we all freeze to death. The next the warm weather is here again, and we're searching for shade.'

'Summer can't come too soon for me.'

'I will remind you of that at Christmas time,' Samantha laughed, and pushed wide the garden gate.

3

As Man to Man

Samantha loved everything about her new life, and Tom realized that it would be a challenge for him to try and catch up with her, and hold his own. She had learned to ride and shoot expertly, and she was prepared to tackle anything. Her mother, it seemed, had given up trying to make her 'behave as a young lady should'.

'It's this wild country,' Aunt Polly bemoaned. 'It is no place for children—or for women either. The men should have tamed it before bringing us here.'

'Oh, Mama, what a lot of fun we would have missed if they'd done so!' Samantha laughed. 'It's really a wonderful life. Just think of it, Tom, there's no school. And during the winter very little work is done by anyone in Pretoria. It's just like one long holiday.'

'You forget that somebody must cook the meals and manage the home, whatever the season,' her mother said tartly.

'And I do my share, Mama, much as I hate housework. You know you could have servants as the other ladies do, and then you could enjoy yourself too.'

'Samantha, don't be pert. This is a barbaric country, and I refuse to have the barbarians in my kitchen, as you well know. What will become of you young people, without education, without culture, running wild with no restraint?'

'Are there really no schools?' Tom could hardly believe it.

'There is talk of starting one, but so far they have no teachers and no school building,' his cousin told him. 'Papa and one or two others do what they can—when they think about it. They occasionally hold classes out of doors. But I assure you, Tom, they have little success. There is always so much of interest to claim our attention. Usually it ends up as a picnic, or someone comes along who has grand tales to tell about the Great Trek or the present Gold Rush, and school's forgotten.'

'But if the men don't work in winter, what do they do?' Tom was trying to get a clear picture of this strange new way of life.

'Oh, they hunt—for the pot, you know, and when rogue beasts come into the district and are a menace; but mostly, I think, for the fun of it, and because hunting is what they depend on for a living. We have wonderful hunts, Tom. Many of the farmers and hunters trek down to the coast with wagons and on horseback before the spring rains make the rivers impassable. They trade their ivory, skins and biltong—that's dried meat—for whatever they need.

'And we all have picnics at the Fountains and the Wonderboom, and at favourite spots along our Apies River—that's the big river that runs through Pretoria. Oh, I'm sure you're going to love it—as I do. And as Papa does. Mama—'

'I can see the dangers, Samantha. That's why I fear and hate this cruel land.'

'But, Mama, surely there are dangers anywhere?' Samantha hesitated, glanced at her cousin, then said very seriously, 'Tom's parents remained safely at home in England, and yet his papa was savagely killed on his farm by a bull, and his mama died of a fever.'

For one painful moment Tom thought his aunt would weep.

'Samantha—I know,' she said sadly. 'I do not have to be reminded of it. But realizing that tragedies can happen anywhere makes this life no less fearsome to me.'

Remembering his aunt as he had known her in England, Tom was shocked by the change in her. Aunt Polly had always been so gay and spirited. She had been very pretty, too, and fond of fine clothes. He remembered once hearing his mother say, 'You make me feel so much a farmer's wife beside you, Polly.' And her sister had laughed and kissed her. 'Is that such a bad thing to feel, dear Ruth? Believe me, the role becomes you.'

Tom's Uncle Andrew had been an attorney in the city of London, and yet he had slipped into this new life as easily and happily as Samantha had done.

Just how well he had adapted himself to the changed circumstances Tom only began to understand when his uncle took him to his office the next day.

As they walked down the middle of the wide main street Tom

thought what a pretty village Pretoria was. Each thatched, white-washed cottage was set in a large garden where an abundance of fruit-trees were already beginning to show signs of spring life, as Samantha had said. Rose hedges continued in almost unbroken lines on either side of the street, behind the furrows, and now that the sun was warm the song of fast-flowing water was ever present. And the lazy crooing of doves.

Tom plied his uncle with questions as they walked along.

'Those Kaffirs working on the furrows, Tom? Those are convicts. You can spot their red shirts a mile away—as easily as the Red Coats. The warder? Oh, he'll be somewhere around no doubt. Probably drinking coffee with a friend. These men never try to escape. That's their prison over there among the trees. Yes, the long red-brick building with the badly thatched roof. They haven't cells, just rows of rough stocks, and the men aren't often locked in them. The warder has mislaid his keys so often that he usually finds it less trouble to forget about the stocks and just to rely on the men not getting lost. Of course with a dangerous criminal it would be different. But there has not been one since we arrived here, to my knowledge. These men are convicted of petty offences, for the most part. They are hired out to do our gardening, as a matter of fact. That was one thing that upset your aunt, until I explained things to the warder and he told any prisoner who came to work for me to leave his prison uniform behind and just come in his khaki trousers.'

'Didn't Pretoria come as a surprise to you, Uncle? I expected a much larger town. You know, being the capital.'

'Frankly, yes, Tom. It was a shock to find it so small and isolated. But the town has grown considerably in the past year. Why, we have five stores and two churches now, and the Volksraad meets here—that's our parliament, you know. It meets over there in that building on Church Square—right in the middle of town.'

Andrew Howes smiled as he watched Tom's reaction to the ramshackle, one-storey thatched building, set in a wilderness of uncut grass and thorn-trees.

'It may not look much, but it's the only building in the Transvaal that is known to the outside world,' he said. 'I have a page on my office wall, torn from the *London Illustrated News*, which shows a photograph of the Volksraad building with three donkeys ruminating in the shade of the veranda. Its caption reads, "At least, in Boerland, they keep their asses out of parliament". But one wonders at times—one wonders.'

They passed a grubby little grog-shop called 'The Hole in the Wall,' the only pub in Pretoria. And a church that was certainly the most impressive building in the town.

Opposite the church was a house, shaded by tall trees. And on the stoep a huge man sat in a Madeira chair, smoking a pipe and

talking to two friends. He wore brown corduroys, and his black serge waistcoat was buttoned up to his neck under his long black jacket. His face was clean-shaven except for a heavy fringe of beard that framed his jaw from ear to ear. He raised his hand in greeting as Mr. Howes called out good morning to him.

Tom had known at once that this was Paul Kruger. He was certainly a mountain of a man, and his loud, deep voice boomed out as though he were addressing a great company of people, instead of his two companions.

It seemed to Tom that his uncle was not anxious to be drawn into conversation with Paul Kruger, and he wondered why this was so when he had written about him with such admiration. Certainly he quickened his pace until they had turned a corner and were out of sound of that foghorn of a voice.

'My office is behind Mr. Henning's store,' Uncle Andrew explained as they approached the little corrugated iron building with the signboard, 'J. Henning. General Dealer.' 'We have an agreement whereby I keep Mr. Henning's books in order, and in exchange I have the use of a room, rent free.'

'Is that part of the barter and exchange arrangement you were telling us about at breakfast yesterday?'

His uncle nodded.

'We carry that as far as it's possible to go, having little ready money between us. We even exchange cardboard I.O.U.s which we call *goodfors*. You will find them in general use—even in the church collection-box. Life is very simple here, Tom. Pretoria's a friendly, tranquil, happy place. If only your aunt—' He swallowed the rest of the sentence in a sigh.

They entered the little store, and Tom was introduced to Mr. Henning and his wife, who were both behind the counter, and to the several customers who lounged there as though time had ceased to matter.

'So this is the young gentleman from London!' Mr. Henning exclaimed. 'Be careful how you cross the streets here, m'lad, or the traffic will sweep you into the sluit and the water'll wash you away!'

'Well, he's survived a postcart ride that beat every record for the run,' one of the men said admiringly. 'Wild Australian digger called Kangaroo Joe was up on the box, and he had those mules pacin' it out like they had a hot poker behind them.'

'Now what could've been his haste, I wonder?' drawled a man who was sitting on a bag of meal sucking an empty pipe.

'Mac Mac,' Andrew Howes said shortly.

'And he won't be the last 'un neither. I do hear there's a trail of diggers marchin' up from D'Urban with the smell o' gold in their noses. Guess we'll be pullin' out ourselves soon enough.'

'Can't go without grub—an' who's got money?'

Mr. Henning pretended not to hear.

'I jest want to be sure this ain't no wild-cat rumour, then I'm hittin' out. I'll barter all I've got here for me swag. Since when have we used money anyway?'

'We get along with little enough of the stuff here in Pretoria,' the storekeeper said dryly. 'But it's real money I have to pay to the merchants in Pietermaritzburg and D'Urban for the goods I barter to you. If money's tight with you, it's mighty tight with me, mate. Don't bank on barter all the way, will you?'

'Come along, Tom.' His uncle led him through the overcrowded store and into a small room at the back. He closed the door, and seated himself behind the desk that took up most of the floor space. 'Open that window, will you, we can do with some fresh air in here.'

Tom was glad to have something to do. He didn't want his uncle to see what a surprise this office had been to him. Tom remembered the elegantly furnished London offices where he had visited his uncle several times. It was hard to believe that this was where his uncle now worked—in this tiny, unlined room, which looked out onto an untidy yard.

'One has to forget the old life, Tom,' his uncle said, pushing his hat onto the back of his head and settling himself more comfortably on his bentwood chair. 'It's like living in a different world out here, and unless one accepts it like that one may as well give up and return to one's native land. No one can live happily with regrets, or wishing conditions were different. I'm going to talk to you as man to man, Tom, and what I say is in confidence between us. Is that understood?'

'Yes, Uncle.'

'I want you to promise me that you will give this country, this new life out here, a year's trial. During that year you must throw yourself into it with everything you have in you, and learn all it has to teach you. And believe me, Tom, there is much that a man can learn here to his advantage.'

'I'm sure of that.'

'If you find, at the end of the year, that this is not the life for you, then I want you to say so frankly, and you will go back to England. Is that agreed?'

Tom nodded. 'I'll remember, Uncle.'

'It means that you will have to learn to shoot and ride like a man. You will have to forget the classroom and take your place among men. Boyhood is soon over in a country like this.'

'May I ask you a few questions, Uncle Andrew? I mean—well, they're rather personal questions.'

'Fire away, Tom. As I said, we are talking now as man to man. Your future will depend upon how you handle your life now. And I only want to help you.' He paused, then added, 'You are the son I never had—put it that way.'

Tom hesitated, obviously embarrassed, then stammered, 'Er—Uncle Andrew—what—what are your circumstances? It sounds strange asking you like that, but I can't help wondering. This office—and all the barter that goes on here, without money. And Pretoria being such a sleepy, poor village. Are you—I mean—'

'What you are asking is how am I fixed, Tom?' His uncle smiled at him, though his eyes were grave. 'I'll tell you, my boy. Things are bad with me. Very bad indeed, in fact. I bought the house we live in, paying cash for it and for the furniture. For the past year I have made practically no money at all, nor am I likely to do so until Pretoria grows in wealth and size. We have been living on my capital since leaving England, and that is almost spent. These are the hard facts, Tom, between ourselves.'

'I understand, and I'm sorry, Uncle.'

'Don't imagine I regret coming out here—insofar as Samantha and I are concerned. It has been a worthwhile experience for us both, whatever happens in the future. But for your aunt it is a different matter. I doubt whether she will ever learn to accept this country, and grow to love it.'

'Have you any plans?'

'As usual, there are two roads we can follow, Tom. We could give up now and return to England. It would mean leaving everything we have here, for I doubt if we could sell our home. I would have to borrow money from my brother in London, and that I do not want to do, for my own good reasons. As you probably know, I sold everything before coming out here, so I would have to begin all over again, which does not attract me, but which I could face if need be.'

'And the other road?'

'Gold, Tom, gold. I believe there are fortunes to be made at Mac Mac. I would give almost anything to be able to try my luck there. It is the chance of a lifetime—my one opportunity to make a great deal of money. Just think what that would mean in terms of security!'

'Have you thought of going to the diggings alone, Uncle, and leaving Aunt Polly and Sam here until you've tried it out?'

'I did think about it, and I suggested it to my wife, but she is too afraid to remain here without me. No, Tom, it would mean all of us going—or none of us.'

They were silent for a time, each deep in his own thoughts.

Suddenly Andrew Howes shook himself out of his mood of anxious depression and smiled across at Tom.

'Well, at least we know what you must do right away, my lad,' he said. 'You must learn to ride and shoot—and that fast. I shall arrange for my good friend, Chris le Roux, to take you in hand and train you for the life here. You are quite unprepared at the moment, and that's a dangerous state of affairs.

'Chris is a farmer—a South African type of farmer, Tom, which is vastly different from the English variety. He grows few crops because the buck and baboons raid them. So he lives by his gun and on his horse, hunting for ivory and skins, and sun-drying the flesh of buck for biltong. He is considered one of the best horsemen and shots in the Transvaal. And he is a fine man. He will train you thoroughly, as he trained Samantha—and me. I warn you that Chris le Roux is tough, and he demands that his time is not wasted. But I know you could not be in better hands.'

'I have never fired a shot in my life,' Tom said dubiously.

'He will understand that. I have a shot-gun which you may use—in fact, it is yours. Samantha and I both have our own guns. And there is a mare waiting for you. You will not find her too spirited, although she has speed.'

'What's her name, Uncle?'

'Star. She has a perfect star on her forehead, so her name was decided for her. As a matter of fact, it is possible that Samantha may be free now, and you could ride together. I suggest you go and see, Tom. You can't start too soon. I have some work to do, and I will send a message to Chris le Roux by a runner at once.'

At the door Tom turned.

'I want to—to thank you, Uncle Andrew,' he said. 'The way you feel about gold—that it offers you the chance of your life—that's the way I feel about the life here. This is my big chance, I know it!'

'Good for you, Tom. It won't be easy, but I believe you'll make good.'

The men were still discussing the Gold Rush when Tom hurried through the shop, and Paul Kruger had apparently not drawn breath; his audience of two still sat bolt upright on their chairs, nodding their heads in agreement at all he said. The only change in the tableau was that they all held cups of coffee now instead of their pipes.

Tom smiled as he remembered Kangaroo Joe's words about Paul Kruger: 'He jest sits and talks, world without end, Amen.'

4
Oom Paul's Rhino

Ten days were to pass before the runner brought Chris le Roux's reply, for he had experienced difficulty in locating the hunting party. And what days of action they had been.

Twice a day Samantha and Tom would saddle up and ride out into the veld.

'Chris will expect you to rough it, Tom,' Samantha had said. 'You will have to ride hard and long. We will get in as much practice as we can before you join up with him, so that you will be prepared, and toughened. You and Star will need to get to know each other's ways, too.'

Riding across the veld was an exhilarating experience, although Tom found it impossible to keep up with his cousin on their first few rides. He had always loved horses, and soon found himself at home in the saddle.

Star was a perfect mount for him, and they suited each other temperamentally. He found he had no need to fear that the mare would fall foul of the many holes and partly submerged boulders, and would throw him. Star was sure-footed and her sight was keen. Tom learned to give her her head and abandon himself to the enjoyment of a hard gallop, without misgivings.

If his muscles were stiff and sore for a day or two from riding, he suffered far more from his introduction to the skill of using a gun. His shoulder was black and blue from the rebound of his rifle, no matter how firmly he held it to him, and he marvelled that a girl like Samantha should have learned to handle her gun with such confidence and accuracy.

'It nearly killed me at first,' she confessed, laughing. 'I felt I could hardly lift the gun, let alone fire it. But I knew I had to learn to shoot, so there was nothing else for it. As Chris kept telling me, a life—perhaps my own—could well depend on how accurately I could handle my gun. And after all most Boer women and girls can shoot, so why shouldn't I?'

Tom was self-conscious about his complete lack of experience, and so they rode some distance out of town for his rifle practice, where Samantha's friends would not hear the shots and gather round to comment and offer free advice.

'It doesn't matter if you can't aim straight at first, Tom,' Sam stressed. 'Nobody is a crack shot in the beginning. But just so that you get over the painful part of learning how to handle and fire your gun before Chris takes charge—that's what counts. You know you don't have to worry about me. I used to be knocked all over the place by the kick of my gun when I first started to learn. My shoulder was black for months. Just relax and bang away. You're going to be a good shot, I'll bet anything on it.'

Tom had grave doubts about that, but he was determined to

master his gun as well as he could. He looked forward to his meeting with Chris le Roux with mixed feelings, if the truth were told, fearing that he would make a fool of himself.

He was certainly not prepared for the handsome, smiling young man who rode up to the gate one day, looking so relaxed in the saddle that he and his horse seemed to be one.

'Chris! Chris!' Samantha cried, rushing from the house to meet him. 'Oh, it's good to see you again.'

Chris had swung down from the saddle, and he scooped Samantha into his arms and gave her a bear hug.

'I hear you held up the postcart and stole—ah, there he is! You are Tom Maxwell?' He held out his hand and Tom's fingers were crushed in his powerful grasp.

Surely this could not be the great hunter Tom had heard so much about? Any misgivings he had nursed vanished in the warmth of Chris's friendly smile.

'I had to come into town so I thought I would call for you, Tom. My business can be finished this afternoon, and we can leave first thing in the morning. Suit you?'

'It certainly does.'

'I'll get coffee while you off-saddle, Chris. Does your horse need water?'

'He can drink at the furrow. Then I'll turn him loose on the commonage for a while. No doubt he can bed down with Meneer Mitchell's beasts for the night.'

Tom watched the man off-saddle and lead his horse to the furrow. He wore corduroys, a khaki flannel shirt and leather jacket, and a leopard-skin band round his wide-brimmed hat.

'You're going to enjoy your first hunt, Tom,' he said. 'We've outspanned over by the Magaliesberg, a large party of us, and the hunting is very good. Of course there are plenty of antelope to be shot anywhere. I'm out for bigger game. Ivory and ostrich feathers, and some giraffe.'

'I'm afraid I'd never fired a gun in my life until a few days ago,' Tom said diffidently. 'I hope you won't find me—'

Chris le Roux slipped off the bridle and slapped his horse's flank, sending him trotting onto the commonage to graze. He hoisted the saddle onto his shoulder and led the way up the garden path.

'Don't you worry your head about that, Tom. Some of us were

lucky enough to have been born in the saddle, as they say, and we've shot ever since we were children. But we don't expect a man to become a good shot overnight. We know what it takes.'

Mrs. Howes came to the front door at sound of their voices, and Tom saw that she was genuinely pleased to see the young hunter.

'Welcome, Christian!' she said. 'You know it says much that I can welcome you even though you ruined my daughter's chances of ever being a young lady. Riding and shooting like a boy, as she does. And now I understand that you are going to make my nephew into a hunter. But welcome, for all that!'

Chris le Roux took her hand and smiled down at her.

'You look very well, and I'm glad to see it, Mevrou Howes,' he said. 'A man must shoot if he is to live in this country. And a woman as well. It remains to decide whether they shoot well, or badly. That is all. And Tom here is going to shoot well. As your husband and Samantha shoot well. And as you will too when you decide to let me teach you.'

'That will never be.'

'A dangerous thing to say, Mevrou. In spite of all you say I recognize a good South African in you. No, don't draw yourself up like that as though I have offended you.' He laughed, his arm about her shoulders. 'I have paid you a great compliment. Please accept it as such.'

'Thank you, Christian. You are quite wrong, of course, but I know you mean it well.'

'I know a little of how you feel because, even though she married a Boer, my mother felt as you do for some years, my father has told me. But in time she found that she could be an English lady and a good South African farmer's wife at the same time. She has learned to love this country as her own. You will get on well together.'

'Coffee's ready!' Samantha called. 'Do you want it on the stoep or indoors, Mama?'

'Indoors, of course, Samantha. You know I cannot get used to eating and drinking in open view of the street. You will want to wash your hands after your ride, Chris? You know your way to the bathroom. Samantha will give you a towel.'

'How I wish I were coming with you two,' Samantha said wistfully as she handed round the cups of coffee and milk rusks.

'Tom and I will be working hard, Samantha,' Chris told her. 'And you know very well what that means. I suggest you stay at home this time like a patient girl and get your mother to teach you to make milk rusks like these. No Boer vrou could better them!'

Samantha giggled delightedly.

'In all honesty I must confess that my daughter made these rusks, not I,' her mother said, smiling. 'You would probably have been served crumpets or scones had I done the baking today.'

It was decided that Tom would meet Christian le Roux at his uncle's office later in the afternoon.

'We must go over your equipment for the hunt, Tom. You may need certain things at the store.'

Samantha and Tom stood at the gate watching Chris stride up the road. He whistled a merry tune, and he walked as though every part of his tall, broad body enjoyed the exercise.

'How is it that he speaks such perfect English?' Tom asked. 'His name—'

'His mother is English, and I believe he had English tutors for some years. Do you like him, Tom?'

'Like him? What a question! He isn't anything like a big-game hunter—at least, he isn't what I imagined a hunter would be like. And he's so young. But he's—he's fine.'

'Yes, he is. He isn't really young at all. Twenty-two. And you'll know he's a hunter all right when you see him in action. He says only a good shot should hunt, because it's a crime to wound an animal. And he hates what he calls "wanton killing". He only shoots for the pot, or for his livelihood.'

'What else would one shoot for?'

'Oh, Tom, don't be silly! You must know that most men just kill for the fun of killing—like target practice. We have often come across dead beasts that have been left to rot in the veld, or wounded beasts that have turned rogue because of their wounds. That kind of thing makes Chris furious.'

'I should think so!'

'You'll see plenty of it, Tom, I assure you. That's one of the reasons why Papa thinks so much of Chris. He says he is humane in a savage land. And he is.'

'Aunt Polly seems fond of him too.'

'Everyone loves Chris. Mama tried hard not to, but she couldn't help herself.'

'Samantha!' her mother called from the house.

'I know what that means—"Come and help me prepare a feast for tonight". You see if I'm not right! You'd better go and warn Papa not to come home too early, Tom. He might miss Chris if he leaves now.'

The afternoon was closing in when the three left Mr. Howes's office for their short walk home.

As they neared Paul Kruger's house the big man stood up and beckoned them over. He was alone, and evidently feeling the need of company.

'Steer clear of all mention of gold, Tom!' his uncle whispered, and Tom understood why they had hurried past the house before.

The two Boers greeted each other in their own language as they shook hands. Paul Kruger clapped his friend on the shoulder, and there was obvious affection between them.

'Sit, sit. I will call for coffee.' Had the kitchen been on the far side of the village, Tom felt sure Paul Kruger's bellow would have been heard. He spoke English quite fluently, with a guttural accent that suited his rugged appearance. 'We will drink coffee together while I hear your news, my friends. This is your nephew, Meneer Howes? I have seen him pass the house. You are well-built, but thin. The life in the veld will soon fill you out and make a man of you. What is your age?'

'Fourteen, sir.'

'A man already, ja? When I was fourteen I shot my first lion—but then I was shooting big game from the age of seven, remember. You can shoot?'

'Tom is coming to the hunt with me in the morning, Oom Paul,' Chris chipped in, straddling a chair and resting his arms on the back.

'And where is this hunt, Christian?'

'Over by the Magaliesberg, Oom. Things go very well. There are seven wagons outspanned there, and several riders have their tents pitched. You know the spot well. You have cause to. It is about two miles north of the place where you shot that rhino.'

'*That* rhino? What rhino may that be? I have shot hundreds of the beasts in my time as you know.'

'But only one that earned you a thrashing, I think.' Chris laughed, and the small blue eyes of the older man twinkled.

'That is one story I have not yet heard,' Andrew Howes said.

A stout middle-aged lady, dressed in a long black dress and with a crocheted shawl over her shoulders, came onto the stoep, followed by an African woman carrying a coffee tray.

'Ah, Tant Sina!' Chris rose to shake hands with Mevrou Kruger.

She nodded at Andrew Howes and Tom, greeting them in Dutch, and left them after she had poured their coffee and the servant had handed it round.

The coffee was so hot and strong that Tom wondered how he would ever drink it. After the first few sips his tongue felt like tanned hide.

'Yes, I will tell you about the rhino that earned me a thrashing. It will be a good lesson for you, Tom, although young men are soft today compared with my youth, and the good, hard old ways have changed.'

Paul Kruger poured his cup of scalding coffee down his throat, placed the empty cup on the floor beside him, and settled back in his chair.

'You must know that in my young days we hunters had an arrangement with each other that if anyone was guilty of reckless carelessness or cowardice on a hunt, he was soundly thrashed. Nobody objected. Why should we? We knew that it was a good thing, and we took our medicine.

'Well, I was out on a hunt with my brother-in-law, Theunissen, who I always thought was too cautious for a hunter. I see now that his caution was sometimes right. But I was always one to rush into danger without proper thought. And I had a sharp lesson to learn.

'I had killed one rhino, while he had wounded another. Without a moment's thought I galloped after the wounded animal.

'"Look out, she's wild," Theunissen shouted. "Don't dismount!"

'But, of course, that is just what I did. I paid no attention to

the warning but jumped off my horse and ran obliquely past the rhinoceros. She had scarcely caught sight of me before she was in hot pursuit. I let her come within a distance of three or four yards. Then I fired. But my percussion cap refused, and there was no time for a second shot.

'The animal was close upon me, and there was nothing to be done but to turn round and run for my very life. In attempting to do so my foot struck against thorn-tree roots, and I came down flat on my face. The beast was upon me; the dangerous horn just missed my back. She had pinned me to the ground with her nose, meaning to trample me to death.

'At that moment I managed to turn under her and got the contents of the second barrel full under the shoulder-blade, right into her heart. I owed my life to not letting go of my hold on the gun during this dangerous adventure. The rhinoceros sprang away from me, but fell down dead a few yards away.

'My brother-in-law hurried up as fast as he could for he thought I had been killed by my own gun in this struggle. But when he saw that I was getting to my feet safe and sound, he took his sjambok and began to belabour me soundly. What could I do? It was according to our hunters' contract, and I had earned that thrashing for acting recklessly, and disregarding his warning. That taught me well!'

Paul Kruger laughed delightedly, but it was as much as Tom could do to twist his face into a smile.

'Don't worry, Tom,' Chris grinned. 'We'll make no such pact, you and I.'

'As I said, times have changed—and not for the better,' their host remarked. 'There are some lessons a man will only learn the hard way.'

'Meneer, that coffee was good. I thank you for the coffee and for the story. But it is getting dark and we should be on our way. Our meal will be waiting for us, and these two must be off at cock-crow.' Andrew Howes held out his hand. 'Good night to you and to Mevrou Kruger.'

'When you return from your hunt I want to see what kind of game you have killed, young man,' Paul Kruger said as he shook Tom's hand. 'You will wear a strip of its skin round your hat as all men do. See that it is not the skin of a meercat!'

'Never fear, Oom Paul,' Chris laughed. 'In Tom here we have a young hunter it will be well to watch.'

'Thanks, Chris,' Tom said when they were out in the road, heading for home and the evening meal. 'I'll probably be lucky to get a meercat, whatever that may be.'

'Never let hunters' talk rattle you, Tom,' his new friend said quietly. 'They're big talkers. You're going to shoot as well as any of them. Just give yourself time and work hard at it.'

5

The Hunt

'Watch Chris—the way he handles his horse and gun. The way he does just everything,' Samantha advised Tom before he rode off at dawn. 'I didn't take my eyes off him when he was training me. It's the only way to learn a hunter's tricks. Everything Chris does looks so easy. It's only when you try to do it yourself that you realize what a wonderful horseman and shot he is.'

Tom hoped he was hiding his true feelings. To himself he admitted that he was badly scared, much as he liked Chris, and in spite of his excitement at the prospect of the hunt. It was not the possible dangers and the thought of roughing it that shook him, but the fear of proving himself hopelessly inadequate when put to the test.

He knew how much he owed Samantha for their days of coaching and practice, and he hoped he wouldn't let her down.

As they trotted out of town through the pearly light and veils of mist Tom felt his heart pound with the conflict of his thoughts and emotions.

'We'll give them a chance to really stretch their legs while there's a road. We'll be branching off into the veld just now,' Chris said, smiling over his shoulder at his companion. 'Horses are always a bit jittery when starting out on a journey.'

'Horses aren't the only ones,' Tom admitted ruefully.

Chris laughed. 'Do you think I don't know how you feel? I've been through it, Tom, although it was a long time ago. The first time one does anything worth while it's a test of guts. Come on—*ride*!' He lifted his reins and pressed his heels into the sides of his big brown horse, who responded immediately by thudding into a gallop.

Several times during their short burst of speed Chris glanced at Tom and his mount. When he pulled in to a canter he was smiling broadly.

'You'll do, man, you'll do!' he cried. 'You're a much better horseman than I expected you to be with so little experience in the saddle. And that mare of yours, she's great. You can relax, Tom, you're doing fine.'

And suddenly Tom was free of the cramp of fear, and wide open to the sheer joy of this wonderful new experience.

It was only when they were stretched out in the shade of a tree with the sun overhead, that Tom realized how much instruction Chris had given him during their hard morning's ride.

Every point he had made had been offered so casually, while they chatted, that Tom had absorbed it easily, and with no build up of anxiety or self-consciousness. Chris had corrected faults in his riding, showing him how to win the best response and performance from his mount, and how to avoid soreness and fatigue in the saddle, and yet he had not seemed to teach him at all.

He had pointed out landmarks and routes, and explained the characteristics of the various game they saw grazing in the vleis or moving in small herds across the veld.

They had rubbed down and watered their horses, which were now knee-haltered and grazing near at hand. Chris and Tom had enjoyed a lunch of cold boerewors (Boer sausage), cheese and brown bread, with dried fruit, and they drank water from the spruit. Aunt Polly and Samantha had packed the saddle-bags with good things for the journey.

'When you've cooled off we're going to put in some gun practice, Tom. The horses aren't yet ready to carry on, but we can't afford to waste time lying here. I thought we would take this journey in easy stages, so that we can get in some practice on the way. Shooting isn't easy. It takes skill and a lot of practice. I refuse to allow anyone I'm responsible for to shoot at game until they're reasonably sure to kill, not wound. And that stands whether they're friends or my hunters.'

'Of course.'

'First of all I want to be sure you can load, aim and shoot smoothly and with confidence. And that takes time and patience. Bullets cost money, so we'll work without them just at first. Then you'll use blanks, and graduate to live bullets when I'm satisfied that you're ready to use them. Right, let's get started.'

The memory of that long ride would remain with Tom throughout his life. Every part of it was a new experience, and much of it tested his nerve, strength and endurance to the limit.

At the end of the first day he ached with exhaustion, and almost fell from the saddle. But there could be no thought of rest until preparations for the night had been made.

'When we've given the horses a rub down we'll take them over to a water-hole not far from here,' Chris said. 'Then we can tether them under these camelthorn trees. The grass is green there —must be a spring somewhere about. We mustn't camp too near the water-hole. The game comes down to drink at night, and it's as well to keep at a safe distance.

'We'll pitch the tents and then we must gather wood for the fire. It has to be kept burning all night to keep prowlers off.' Chris slapped Tom's shoulder, smiling into his tired face. 'And then it's grub, man, and a good night's sleep.'

Fortunately there was an abundance of dry wood within easy range, and Chris chopped down a dead tree, dragging the trunk to their camp on the side of a little koppie overlooking the vlei.

In a surprisingly short time the tent was pitched, the fire was burning, and Chris was stirring coffee and sugar into the billy-can of spluttering water balanced on small boulders over the flames.

'Get those chickens and mealie bread out of your saddle-bag, Tom. Let's have your mug—this coffee smells good. Coffee's always better if it's stirred with a burnt stick like this. Gives it flavour.'

Although Tom had thought himself too tired to eat, he finished a whole roast chicken, washed down with two mugs of sweet, strong coffee.

'You turn in,' Chris said, yawning. 'I'll roll up by the fire. Have to keep an eye on the horses and make sure the fire doesn't die down during the night.'

'We'll take it in turn, it's only fair,' Tom insisted.

'All right. You've got to get the experience some time. I'll call you to take over later on then.'

Tired as he was, Tom slept fitfully. His first deep sleep was shattered by an eerie, high-pitched scream, followed by what sounded like human sobs, groans and more screams. He stumbled out of the low tent and stood staring about him. The fire was still burning brightly, and beside it Chris was rolled in his blankets, as still as a log.

Without moving, or showing any other sign that he was awake, Chris said:

'Only a hyena, Tom. All's well.'

'It sounded—human.' Tom's teeth were chattering from cold and shock.

'You'll get used to it. Night's busy time—in the veld. Sleep!'

But sleep didn't come easily, although body and brain ached for it. The night was loud with strange and sinister sounds. Several times the horses whinnied and stamped in fright, and Chris called out to them in reassurance, and once fired into the air to frighten off a marauder.

When Tom eventually gave up all hope of sound sleep, and went to take his turn of watch by the fire, he found that Chris had built up a second fire on the far side of the horses. Again, although he didn't move, Chris proved that he was wide awake when Tom approached the fire.

'Haven't you slept at all, Chris?'

'Of course. I've had a good night.' He yawned and stretched. 'One learns to sleep lightly, that's all. Anything wrong, Tom?'

'I'm going to take my watch—give you a break.'

'Right. Doss down near the fire. Other side.'

'Won't you sleep in the tent now, Chris?'

'I'll stay here. Always sleep out. 'Night.'

Tom found a slight depression and curled up in it, rolling himself into a cocoon in his thick brown blankets. The warmth of the fire relaxed his stiff body and gently thawed his face.

It was the delicious smell of coffee that awoke him. To his shame he had slept like a log.

'Forget it,' Chris laughed, when Tom stammered an apology. 'You'll learn to sleep lightly. It takes time. Come on, grub's ready.'

They ate thick mealie meal porridge and sugar, and drank their coffee. Afterwards Tom carried the plates and mugs to the water-hole to wash them, while Chris led the horses to drink.

As though it were a page from a book, Chris read the crazy pattern of hoof and paw imprints in the mud round the water's edge. He casually explained to Tom that two lions had been there during the night, as well as various kinds of buck, quagga, a family of warthogs, and at least one giraffe.

The sun was just flushing the sky, and there was great twitter and busyness among the small birds, and cries from the coranne and partridge as they took to the air.

'While the horses graze you can get in some gun practice,' Chris said, as they struck camp. 'You've got to learn to shoot in every kind of light, Tom. Light can play tricks with one, and a hunter must learn about those tricks.'

For three days and two nights they rode, shot, camped, slept

and talked. They chewed springbok biltong between meals as they rode, and once Chris shot a guinea-fowl. Drawing it, he caked it with red clay, and roasted it in the glowing embers of their fire. When it was ready he cracked the hard case that covered the bird, and the feathers fell away with the clean, baked clay. Tom declared that he had never eaten such a tender, tasty bird.

For Tom the days were packed with discovery and adventure. He soon learned that nothing could be taken for granted; the unexpected kept him alert and interested. He loved the hard days in the open, the challenge to give of his best, and the company of Christian le Roux, whose love and knowledge of wild life provided Tom with a perfect introduction to the creatures of veld and air that constantly intrigued him.

By the second night he had been so exhausted that he not only slept through the usual weird and disturbing night sounds, but he even rolled over and slept again almost immediately after the roar of a lion had reverberated across the veld, to be followed by a period of tense silence before the night symphony again settled on the world.

'Oh, you're not the heaviest sleeper I've known,' Chris laughed, when Tom despaired of learning to sleep lightly enough to be trusted to take his turn on night watch. 'At one of our camps there was a farmer named van Rooyen who slept like the dead. One night a lion actually walked into his tent, grabbed his foot, and dragged him out into the veld. Man, you've never heard anything like van Rooyen's yells; the lion was so scared it bolted before any of us could get a shot at it.'

When at last they reached camp early one evening, Tom sat his horse with new confidence. In more ways than one he had come a long, long way in the past three days.

The camp was situated on a plateau in the foothills of the towering Magaliesberg mountains, with a river near at hand and a magnificent view which tantalized in the waning light. Deep purple shadows smudged the distance, and cushions of cloud, caught on the peaks, were spilling drifts of feathers down the mountain-sides.

The wagons had been outspanned to form the customary 'laager' circle, in the centre of which there was now great activity as fires were lit and the evening meals prepared. The air was already blue with wood smoke, and the smell of meat roasting over glowing embers made Tom's mouth water.

Oxen were being driven into their kraal a short distance from the camp, the cries of the herd boys and lowing of the cattle adding to the pleasant, welcoming chorus of voices and evening sounds that greeted the travellers. A thickly matted wall of thorn-tree branches encircled the kraal, as protection from night marauders.

Chris and Tom dismounted before they reached the wagons, and almost at once a young Native man appeared beside them, his eyes reflecting the smile with which he welcomed Chris. Tom wished that he understood the animated conversation that followed between them, and made a private vow that he would not only learn to speak Dutch, but the language of the local Native tribesmen as well.

'This is Kameel, Tom, the finest hunter I've ever had,' Chris said, handing the reins of his horse to the man and indicating that Tom should do the same. 'He will take care of the horses.'

As they walked into the circle of the camp Chris was welcomed on all sides, and Tom felt particularly glad at that moment to be his friend. What better introduction could he have had to these strangers?

To Tom's surprise only Dutch was spoken. In Pretoria English had been in general use, but here, he very soon realized, he was faced with a language problem.

Lanterns were being lit and hung on wagons and the branches of trees, and there was much laughter and shouting and banter.

Most of the women wore white aprons to protect their long, full skirts, and the men who sat about resting and smoking their pipes after the day's hunt, or who supervised the many jobs that must be attended to before nightfall, wore the game-skin breeches or stiff corduroys, velskoen and leather jackets, common among hunters and farmers. The young people dressed much as their parents did, and many of them stared at Tom with open curiosity as though summing him up before extending their friendship. He didn't know that he wore a very similar mask of unsmiling caution, and that they misread his shyness as he did theirs.

'Kameel tells me that there's a surprise awaiting us at the wagon,' Chris said as he and Tom slowly made their way across the busy camping ground.

'Chris, doesn't anyone here speak English?'

His friend shook his head. 'I hardly think so. Some of them may know a little English, but they very seldom use it. You see it's only in the towns that you hear it spoken—and on the diggings, of course. Few of our people are attracted to the diamond and gold-mines. We're farmers, people of the land, and hunters. But don't worry, Tom, I'll help you out. We'll be off hunting most of the time, and, believe me, it won't be long before you pick up our language. Sammy learned it very quickly, and you will, too.'

He stopped short with an exclamation. There, stretched out to dry on the tilt of the wagon before them, was the skin of a large, black-maned lion. A magnificent specimen.

'Kameel!' Chris shouted, and strode off to find his Native hunter. When he rejoined Tom his eyes were shining.

'That Kameel!' His laugh didn't hide the pride in his voice. 'Do you know, Tom, he went out after this lion when it had been wounded by another hunter—tracking it alone in very bad light. He didn't give up until he finally trailed it to a ravine smothered in dense bush. And he shot it dead as it sprang out at him maddened by its wound. That took courage. But Kameel has plenty of it. The three of us will be off in the morning. From what he says it promises to be an exciting hunt—you may even get your meercat for Oom Paul!'

As they were laughing a man joined them, clapping Chris on the shoulder as the two men chatted, and including Tom in his warm smile of welcome.

'Meet my good friend and neighbour, Piet du Toit, Tom. He's just invited us to eat with his family. Now you're really going to taste food for a man—braaied quagga steaks and sweet potatoes.'

What a meal that was! Sitting relaxed round the fire, on chairs, or logs or the ground, each one helping himself to the chops that sizzled on a grid over the fire, and spearing roasted sweet potatoes from the hot embers, his tin plate balanced on his knees. Tom felt himself drawn into the heart of that big, friendly family, even though he could only communicate by smile and gesture. It was enough for them that he was Chris le Roux's friend, that he enjoyed their food, and returned their smiles.

Chris drew Tom into the circle of talk whenever possible, quick to interpret and explain to him. The meal over, Chris went off to find a lad of about Tom's age, who could understand and speak a certain amount of English, so Piet du Toit had said.

'Tom, this is Jacob.' Chris introduced the obviously reluctant youth he had in tow. 'Jacob has lived in Pretoria for a time, so he understands English. See how you two get on together.'

But Jacob was a silent type and not given to easy chatter in any language. After making a few futile attempts to strike up conversation with him, Tom gave up. Jacob either didn't understand English at all, or he just didn't want to talk. They lapsed into heavy silence, and presently Jacob muttered an excuse and made his escape when Chris's attention was engaged elsewhere. Tom didn't mind. From his own uncomfortable experience he recognized shyness such as Jacob's, and in any case his eyes were closing and his brain felt drugged with exhaustion, the heavy meal, and the warmth of the fire.

Suddenly he was roused by a new tide of activity and excitement that washed around him, sweeping him from his comfortable log as the centre of the camping ground was cleared and large bucksails were spread over the grass.

'There's going to be dancing.' Chris shouted the explanation across to Tom from where he was caught up in conversation with a group of friends.

So that he would be out of the way, and also to command a good view of the dancing, Tom climbed up onto Chris's wagon and made himself comfortable on the driver's seat.

Two young men were trying out chords on their concertinas, while a third blew a few experimental notes on a mouth-organ. Then, with a flourish, they swung into a gay dance tune, and at once the couples began to crowd onto the bucksail dance floor. They danced as they did everything else, with great gusto, the young men often swinging the girls off their feet, and lookers-on clapping in rhythm and calling out praise and encouragement to the dancers.

It didn't surprise Tom that Chris was one of the first on the floor, or that he danced with the prettiest girl there. She was a lovely, laughing girl, whose black curls spread out in a fan behind her head as Chris spun her round and round. Her full, long red dress flickered like a flame whenever they passed near a lantern and the light played over them.

They made such a handsome, happy pair that Tom's eyes followed them until his head felt dizzy. Where did Chris get all his energy? he wondered.

They were still dancing with the same enthusiasm when Tom fell asleep in the wagon, deaf to the rollicking music and laughter, as he had been the previous night to the screams of hyenas, hooting of owls and the lion's roar.

It was still very dark when Chris awoke him.

'Kameel has made the coffee and everything's ready, Tom. Wake up, man, we've got a big day ahead.'

'But it's the middle of the night—'

'Don't you believe it. There's first light in the sky already. The sun will be up before long. This is your first real hunt, Tom. You've never experienced anything like it, I promise you that.'

There was a tension and excitement in Chris's voice that communicated itself to Tom. With a bound he was out of his blankets and had jumped down from the wagon. For a minute he stood stretching his arms above his head as he gulped in the cold, bracing mountain air.

A mug of coffee was passed to him, and in the soft light of a lantern Tom saw the smiling face of Kameel. Their eyes held. Here was a man one could trust and follow, Tom thought. A different race, a different language, what did it matter? Here was a brave man who could teach him much.

Far away, like a faint echo of thunder, came a lion's roar.

'Meercat!' Tom thought, and a laugh rose in his throat. Oh, this was the life all right.

6

The Ghost and the Kudu

A few others were stirring in camp, and fires were being kindled, by the time the three rode out.

As they trotted, close together, Chris explained, 'When Kameel returned to camp yesterday he'd left two of our hunting parties out in the veld. We're going to check on them first. One party's making its way back to camp on foot, with a load of skins and feathers. The other—'

'Feathers?' Tom was surprised.

'Ostrich feathers. They're about the most valuable prize a hunter can bring in, apart from ivory. Thank heaven for the vanity of women! Do you know, Tom, a male ostrich carries a good £10 worth of feathers, and a female about £4. Some hunters go after nothing else, there's such a demand overseas for ostrich feathers. But they're talking of imposing a very stiff fine for mass slaughter of these birds because they're in danger of being wiped out.

'The other men are trailing a herd of elephants. That's why I've brought along my heavy old elephant-gun as well.'

They rode in companionable silence for a while. Tom was very conscious of the sights and sounds of the awakening world about him. There was a grandeur about dawn out there in the veld that he had never before known. The immense sky sheltering the world gradually came alive with gentle and then blazing colour, just as the veld awoke to the faint, tentative twitter of birds, and suddenly broke into a loud, grand chorus of song and sound. The rustle of the dawn wind, as it blew softly over the tall, dry grass, rose to a sweet, steady, flute-like sound as one rode against it, before it died away presently with a sigh into the valleys.

There was magic in that brief hour of the world's awakening. And it was evident that all three riders felt it, for they were caught up together in silence as they watched it, and rode into the growing sound and light of the morning.

Only when the horses had carefully picked their way over the stony bed of a spruit, which was running low, and were climbing the far bank, did Chris speak again.

'A hunter's life's pretty wonderful, Tom,' he said slowly. 'But there are times when it hurts to kill. Hurts like hell.' He turned and looked at his companion to see if he understood what he was trying to confide. 'There's always this feeling of sadness when I'm going out after ivory. Elephants are grand creatures. There's a nobility about them. To shoot them down for their tusks—! But it's part of life. Part of this game we're all playing—hunters and hunted.' For a while they rode again in silence. Then Chris laughed shortly. 'Yes, I suppose that's what it is,' he said, as though following a train of thought out loud. 'I'm a farmer at heart, not a hunter at all. I want to grow things. Trees and grain.'

'Then why—?'

'It's what I've just said, Tom. The hunters and the hunted. We don't always play the same role, you know. I've tried twice to make a go at farming. But the wild things beat me. They eat my crops and kill my stock. So now I have to be the hunter, in order to live. But some day the balance will be more even. I'll be able to grow my wheat and mealies and fruit, and breed my cattle and sheep in some sort of peace. Everything in its proper time, I suppose, as my father always reminds me.'

So that was what Aunt Polly had meant when she said that the men should have tamed the land before bringing the women and children to live there? It was a big thought. Too big to be puzzled over at the moment. But he knew that he agreed with Samantha—they would have missed a lot of fun if the dangers and hardships had all been overcome before they arrived on the South African scene.

'There aren't any camels in this part of Africa, are there?' Tom asked suddenly.

'Camels?' Chris laughed at the unexpectedness of the question. 'That's about the only creature we haven't got here, Tom. Camels and polar bears. Mind you, I've heard they've recently brought a few camels down to the Lowveld from up north, just as an experiment—for transport, I suppose. Why on earth do you ask?'

'Isn't that what Kameel's name means? It seems obvious.'

Chris laughed again, and explained Tom's question to Kameel, who shared his laughter.

'Kameel means giraffe in the Venda language. Look at this fellow's long neck, and you'll understand how he got his name!'

'Well, I've learnt my first Venda word, anyway—"kameel", giraffe,' Tom smiled. 'Tell me, Chris, do most hunters feel the way you do about killing elephants?'

'Of course not! They'd think me mad if I tried to tell them how I feel about it. Hunting's a passion with most Transvaalers, Tom. It's not only their means of livelihood, it's their main sport as well. Most of them think no more of killing an elephant than of wringing the neck of a fowl. Perhaps it's best that way—although I wonder. Feeling the way I do gives me some uncomfortable moments, but at least it makes me feel responsible about always shooting to kill—and seeing that my hunters do, too. I think we'll call a halt by that water I see shining over there. It's time to eat, and rest the horses.'

They rode away from the towering mountains, out into the plains. Game was so plentiful that, at a distance, the blesbok, kudu, wildebeeste, and those close cousins the zebra and quagga, looked like herds of grazing cattle. The smaller springbok and duikers were even more plentiful. Only when the riders drew within range did the buck drift or race away.

And, against the sun-bleached sky, there was always at least one eagle, seemingly motionless, with wings outstretched and gaze pin-pointed on the veld below, among the gliding, sweeping, darting birds that wove a constantly changing pattern of movement overhead.

It was late afternoon when they met Chris's hunting party, the men walking in single file.

First came the three hunters with their guns, and behind them eight bearers balancing great loads of hides, horns and feathers on their heads. The loads were securely bound with thick ropes of woven grass and reed, and the men chanted a song as they walked. Sweat ran down their faces and bodies, and they moved with a curious, shuffling, rhythmical gait, covering the ground at deceptive speed. Some of the bearers carried short stabbing spears in their hands, others sticks, and all of them were smiling and in high spirits. It had obviously been a good hunt, and the sweat and labour were just part of the day's experience.

Tom studied the men while Chris and Kameel talked to the hunters. He marvelled that they could carry such weights on their heads with perfect poise.

Presently Chris swung his horse alongside Tom's, and Kameel raised his hand in salute before falling in at the head of the file of men who resumed their march.

'Kameel will camp with the men tonight and rejoin us in the morning,' Chris explained. 'Apparently there's a party of our people encamped about a mile farther on. We'll join it, Tom.'

Flocks of white egrets were beginning to roost for the night on the tops of thorn-trees, looking like heavy falls of snow.

Tom commented on the beautiful sight the birds made as they flew in shining arrow formations across the veld, to alight on their favourite roosting trees.

'Most people call these egrets "tick birds", but they're wrong,' Chris said. 'The real tick bird's small and brownish-grey with a red beak. It's a funny sight to watch them pick the teeth of crocodiles. The crocs dose with their mouths wide open so that their teeth can be cleaned by the birds.'

A thin column of smoke led them to the camp, and they found a wagon outspanned near a spring, with a tent pitched a short distance away.

They were given a warm welcome by the family who were making themselves comfortable for the night and preparing their evening meal. To Tom's relief they spoke English. Their name was Williams, and they were on their way to Pretoria after a disastrous attempt at farming. Mr. and Mrs. Williams had three

small children with them, and looked worn out by the trials of the past year, spent battling against impossible odds out in the wilds.

'They warned us that it was madness trying to farm on our own,' Mr. Williams confessed. 'But I had to learn the hard way I suppose. I was a schoolmaster in England, but always wanted to travel, and I had been brought up on a farm. It seemed that this country offered just what I wanted—to farm in a new land. Well, now we're going right back to England as quickly as possible, and very glad we will be to reach civilization again. My poor wife, especially. This has been a terrible ordeal for her.'

A rough-looking character emerged from the tent and slowly approached them. His features were hidden by ginger whiskers, and the brim of his wide, battered felt hat was pulled low on his brow.

Tom's heart leapt at sight of him. Here, surely, was a digger. A man like Kangaroo Joe. When he came nearer Tom saw that he had the same fiercely blue eyes, and that they shone with the almost fanatical fire he had so often seen light up the eyes of his friend.

Mr. Williams introduced the newcomer. 'Meet Rollingstone Charlie, a geologist who is spending a night with us. Christian le Roux and Tom Maxwell, Charlie.'

The man shifted the rock he carried from his right hand to his left, and nearly pulverized Tom's fingers in his powerful handshake.

'Glad to meet you,' he mumbled. Then, his voice suddenly ringing clear as a bell, 'Heard any news of the diggings, mates?'

'You mean Mac Mac?' Chris asked, giving as good as he got as he wrung the man's hand.

'Sure I mean Mac Mac. Pack o' lies, d'you think, or is there some truth in it?'

'Oh, I'd say there is gold there all right. I don't know anything about gold, mind you, but I happened to see some samples of conglomerate reef a digger brought to Pretoria to be crushed. He was from Mac Mac. Everyone seemed very excited about it, if that's any guide.'

The blue eyes burned more brightly than ever.

'That's what I heard, mate, that's it. I'm on my way down there now.'

'What's that in your hand?' Tom asked, intrigued by the jagged stone that shot purple flashes as the light caught it.

'This? Amethyst. Tons of the stuff around here. You want it or something?' He held it out to Tom.

'Do you mean you're giving it to me?'

'What else? I jest happened to crack this rock open a moment ago. Other half's in my tent if you want it. No use to me, boy. I'm only interested in one thing—gold!'

'Well, thanks. Thank you very much. I hope you find your gold.'

The stone was like a split pomegranate, the lilac and purple amethysts clustered within it.

'You will eat with us, won't you?' Mrs. Williams invited them all. 'I have made a big stew, more than enough for everyone. You're very welcome.'

As darkness gathered they settled down to a happy meal round the fire. Tom took one child on his knee and fed him. And soon the children were all fed and asleep in the wagon, and Mr. and Mrs. Williams relaxed by the fire, obviously glad of the company.

They had encountered every kind of disaster in their brave efforts to create a farm in the wilderness.

'We were even plagued by ghosts,' Mr. Williams declared. 'I know it sounds insane, but it is a fact. There was a cave on the farm, and on certain nights apparitions would appear from the mouth of the cave and fly down the hill-side to the farm. They stopped at nothing. I assure you it is true. My wife and I saw them twice with our own eyes. It was no rumour spread by the Kaffirs. We actually saw them!'

'What did they do?' Chris asked seriously.

'They stole our cattle. Drove them off before our eyes. The cattle used to stampede in terror, and while we were trying to prevent them from all escaping to their deaths, these—these ghosts would take off with one or two of our beasts.'

'Did you ever shoot at the ghosts, Mr. Williams?'

'Of course. But it had no effect whatever.'

'I think,' his wife said sadly, 'I really think that was the last straw that broke my husband's spirit. He could fight natural afflictions, and he did—nobly. But—supernatural? We realized that this country was no place for us, or for our dear children. We left while we still had enough oxen to draw our wagon.'

'It reminds me of the White Horse Ghost,' Chris said slowly. 'Perhaps you have heard of it?'

None of them had, it seemed, and they pressed Chris to tell them about it.

'You saw this—this White Horse Ghost yesself, mate?' Rollingstone Charlie asked cautiously.

Chris shook his head.

'It was a bit before my time, but my father vouches for it. And, believe me, my father isn't easily convinced about such things. But wait till you've heard the story.

'It happened in the district of Swellendam, in the Cape Colony. My father was a young man at the time, and there are others still living who were concerned in it I believe.

'The farmers of the Cape were troubled by robber bands and raids by the dreaded Xosas who spread terror throughout the Colony. But this ghost was something quite new in their experience, and it caused such widespread panic that it threatened to disorganize the road traffic completely between Cape Town and Swellendam. A serious business.

'They said it was a ghost which appeared in the form of a large white horse. It made its first appearance in the moonlight, suddenly riding down on a wagon which was outspanned for the night.

It was pure white, and though it whinnied, its hoofs made no sound. To the terrified traveller and his servants the creature seemed to float through the air, and they huddled together, too afraid to stir from the safety of the wagon until the following morning.

'Although the apparition had circled the wagon several times, there was no trace of a horse's hoof imprints to be found. The ghostly visitor had stolen nothing, and had done no harm apart from scaring these men almost out of their wits.

'The next appearance of the white horse had far worse consequences. It happened a week later, the horse descending upon a man who was travelling by spider, accompanied by a single Hottentot servant, and carrying a large sum of money. They were sleeping in the open, and when the horse appeared they fled to a deserted hut where they stayed all night. In the morning they found that the money was missing from the spider.

'This was the first of many robberies. They always happened on a moonlight night, and when the horse vanished so did money or valuables. Whites and blacks alike fled at sight of the horse, and there was never a spoor or a clue of any kind when they returned.

'At last the mystery was solved by the courage of a man named Carl Pohl. He confessed that he was afraid of the white horse that moved with complete silence apart from its whinnying, and left no hoof-prints. But something had to be done to clear up the mystery.

'With the utmost secrecy he took into his confidence only four of his friends and two Hottentots whom he could trust implicitly. He spread word that he was taking a loaded wagon to Cape Town, and ridiculed the notion that there was a ghost in the form of a white horse.

'Well, nothing happened on the outward journey. Carl Pohl sold his goods in Cape Town and at once set out for Swellendam. One moonlight night they outspanned at a carefully chosen spot, and the men gathered round the camp fire. Each man carried a gun and knew what he must do if the horse appeared. Only if their lives were in danger were they to shoot.

'Suddenly they heard a distant whinnying call, and the terrifying apparition of the white horse appeared about sixty yards away. Carl gave the order to run for it—but most of the men had already taken to their heels.

'Abruptly, Carl Pohl and his friends turned and rushed to outflank the horse, with the Hottentots closing in despite their terror. The horse tried to escape, but it was surrounded. The whinnying ceased and it became evident even to the Hottentots that the creature was of flesh and blood, although a large bulge beneath its belly puzzled everyone. A noose was secured round its neck, then a second noose, and as the men forced the animal closer to the fire, to their astonishment a small man, dressed all in white, appeared to drop from beneath the horse.

'With great agility he tried to slip through the cordon, but was tackled and brought to the ground. And the mystery of the White Horse Ghost was solved.'

'But how?' Mrs. Williams asked breathlessly.

'A white cloth was wound round the animal's body with just sufficient space to allow a small man to lie inside it, under the horse's belly,' Chris explained. 'The horse was trained so that the little Hottentot robber could guide it while lying in that position. It was the man who made the whinnying sounds.'

'But you said there were no hoofprints—'

'True. The horse's hoofs were covered with thick raw-hide shoes with the hair on the outside, while the man's feet were muffled in sacking.'

'And that story is true?' Mr. Williams demanded.

'Quite true. I can give you the names of the men who helped Carl Pohl lay that ghost. They are my father's friends. Hottentots are the cleverest thieves in the world.'

'It could have been that a somewhat similar trick was played on me,' Mr. Williams said slowly. 'There were Hottentots in the district, of course. Yes, that could be the explanation, you know.'

'Although nothing would induce me to return to the farm, this has eased my mind.' Mrs. Williams smiled at her husband. 'The thought that they were ghosts has disturbed me deeply. Perhaps in time we will be able to laugh at our terror. It seems unlikely now—but given time—'

'Before we leave these good people there's something I want you to do, Tom,' Chris said the next morning.

'Yes?'

Chris laid a hand on Tom's shoulder and looked at him squarely.

'We have eaten their food. I suggest you shoot for their pot, Tom. Your first kill. Do you think you can do it?'

'Do you?'

Chris nodded.

'I know you can, Tom.'

'Now?'

'Now. Go alone. I'll come when I hear your shot. There always has to be a first time for everything. Good luck, Tom.'

When the shot rang out Chris held his breath for one long moment of time. But there was no second shot. He found Tom standing beside the body of a magnificent kudu bull.

Chris flung an arm round the boy's shoulders and gave him a brief, hard hug.

'I couldn't have done a cleaner job, Tom. Good for you.'

Tom dragged his gaze from the dead beast at his feet and met his friend's understanding eyes.

'I know how you feel about—elephants,' he said. 'I don't think I'm a born hunter either, Chris.'

7

The Ivory Trail

They turned in their saddles to wave and look their last on the friends they had made overnight.

'It's strange, you know, Chris,' Tom said. 'I feel I've known them all my life. They're friends. Rollingstone Charlie—I wonder if he'll find his gold, and meet Kangaroo Joe? And the Williamses—do you think they really will return to England?'

'I wonder. But I know what you mean. We're drawn together like this by the perils and hardships we share here, Tom. They expose a man's real nature. His strengths and weaknesses. We're so dependent on one another in this land that we recognize friends and enemies very quickly. I've heard my mother say that in England people can live as near neighbours for a lifetime and not pass the time of day. But here—well, it's a case of "Hail, stranger—welcome, friend".'

'Yes, it's like that. I say, Sam's going to like this chunk of amethyst, isn't she?' They rode in easy silence for a while. Then Tom asked, 'By the way, Chris, did you hear that lion roaring last night? I wonder if we'll see it? It sounded quite near.'

Chris laughed.

'That wasn't a lion—it was an ostrich,' he said.

'Oh, no! The roar I heard was a lion all right.'

'Even experienced hunters often mistake the *brom* of an ostrich for a lion's roar. The female has no voice at all. She's dumb. But the male bird makes up for her. He roars just like a lion. It's part of their defence—scares other animals off.'

Tom looked unconvinced. He suspected that Chris was joking. But he was soon to learn his mistake.

They rode hard and long that morning. Twice they met parties of Native hunters and bearers returning with their loads, but none of them had news of Chris's men, or of the elephant herd they trailed.

'When my father was a young man there were great herds of elephants on these plains,' Chris explained to Tom. 'But they've been ruthlessly wiped out. Soon there won't be any in these parts at all. Hunters are already having to hunt down in the Lowveld for elephants, in spite of the danger of fever.'

It was the next day before they caught up with his bearers, the hunters having gone on ahead. Chris briefly inspected the two sets of tusks the men carried with their other spoils of the hunt, while he questioned them.

'It seems the hunters have pressed on after an old tusker,' Chris said. 'The poor beast has been injured—in a fight or by a bullet, they don't know the cause. But it has dropped out of the herd, apparently, and it's savage with pain. We'll go on at once. They can't be very far ahead now.'

It was Kameel who first sighted the vultures massing in the sky.

'They know the old fellow is doomed, and they're gathering for the kill,' Chris said. 'Now that we know just where it is we can move up against the wind so that it doesn't get our scent.'

Chris handed his rifle to Kameel to carry while he loaded his 4.65 double-barrelled Magnum Express, ready for action.

'Keep back a bit, Tom. Kameel and I will have to deal with this one, and a pain-maddened elephant can present problems when it's cornered.'

They met their hunters on the edge of a mopani thicket. The men were obviously relieved to leave the killing to Chris and Kameel for they were tired from their long hours of foot-tracking. The animal was a giant, they said, and in ugly temper.

'We'll dismount and leave the horses with these men,' Chris said. 'Will you remain with them, Tom?'

'I'd rather come along with you.'

Chris nodded his agreement, and the three set out, walking in single file, in silence, and alert for the first sight of the wounded beast.

Chris had explained to Tom that only a fool would venture to shoot an elephant from the front, unless necessity forced the decision. Then one would aim between the eyes. But this would seldom kill. The surest shot was from the animal's side, behind the shoulder, into the heart and lungs. Behind the eyes, from the side, was also a good shot, but the target was much smaller.

Tom could sense Chris's tension as they cautiously advanced through the trees.

There was not a sound. Even the crickets and birds were silent. Tom felt his heart thud with excitement. The hunters had said that the old bull was hiding out in the thicket, and Chris had once told him how an elephant could become almost invisible, standing motionless in the shadow of trees. But surely so large a creature . . . ?

Suddenly there was a noise like thunder as the elephant trumpeted its rage and bore down upon them. Everything went before it. Trees were snapped off or uprooted. It seemed to loom directly

before and above them, and Tom made a wild dive for the thick trunk of a tree to the right.

The report of Chris's gun seemed to shake the earth. There was a terrible sound, part scream part bellow, from the stricken beast, and then Tom saw it crash to the ground and lie still.

It had taken only one shot to dispatch it. That, at least, was some comfort.

And, almost at once, came the cries of the native hunters as they rushed the thicket, their tiredness forgotten.

'Look at that foot!' Chris's voice was hard with anger. 'It's been caught in one of the diabolical traps these Vendas set for them. Poor brute! It must have suffered hell. We can be thankful that it's out of its agony.'

Tom couldn't bear to look at the mangled, gangrenous foot of the giant. Instead, he found his attention riveted on swarms of tiny brown ants that were already climbing onto the still warm body.

'Kameel will see to the rest of it. Come on, Tom. Let's get back to the horses and make some coffee. It's a long time since last we ate or drank.'

As they drank their coffee they watched the vultures mass in the sky and spiral in ever lowering circles until they began to alight on the tops of the mopani trees, sitting with hunched shoulders and repellent blood-red necks, watching the men as they worked below on the carcass.

'First the vultures, then the Natives will begin to arrive from far and near. They watch the sky and follow these loathsome birds. And then the jackals and hyenas and wild dogs. Ah, well, that's how Nature works. Someone had to put it out of its misery. And those tusks should weigh quite eighty pounds each. A grand old tusker he must have been.'

'What do you think he weighed, Chris?' Tom asked, still amazed at the towering bulk of the creature that had borne down on them.

'Oh, I'd say quite six or seven tons. It will surprise you to see how quickly that mountain of flesh vanishes when men and predators get busy.'

'Are you going after the rest of the herd, Chris?'

After a moment's thought, Chris shook his head.

'No, Tom. I've had enough of the ivory trail for a while. The bearers will be along before dusk, and we can leave the job to these men now. Ah, there's Kameel. He can ride with us. He isn't needed here either. This will be a noisy place tonight. We'll camp out of earshot of the feasting.'

When the roar shook all other sounds to silence and echoed back from the koppie below which they were camped for the night, Tom sat up as though, even in deep sleep, he had been waiting for the sound.

'Chris! Chris—did you hear that?' he demanded.

There was no movement from the figure curled up on the far side of the fire. But Chris laughed.

'I heard it all right. What do you think it is, Tom?'

'*Think?* It's a lion.'

'Wrong. An ostrich. Care to bet on it?'

With a sigh that ended in a prodigious yawn, Chris sat up.

'Look here, you don't have to take my word for it. But I'm sure I'm not going to get out in the cold to convince you. *Kameel!*'

At once there came the soft answering voice of the hunter. Chris and he exchanged a few words, and Kameel joined them. He carried his gun.

'It's the devil trying to see an ostrich at night—the male's black and white. But there is some moonlight. I vote you and Kameel go out after this one. Don't take your gun, Tom. Only a very experienced hunter should shoot in dim light like this. Leave it to Kameel. Stay close to him, and make as little noise as possible.'

Tom didn't need a second invitation. He had already pulled on his boots and jacket. Without a word he followed Kameel beyond the ring of firelight, after grinning at Chris. The grin said, 'Ostrich—or lion? We'll see!'

Although he still believed he had heard a lion, he knew that, whether they hunted lion or ostrich, he could rely on Kameel to see him safely through the experience. He had no fear.

As his eyes grew accustomed to the quivering light of crescent moon and brilliant stars, Tom fell completely under the spell of the night. From afar he could hear the maniacal laughter and screams of jackals and hyenas, and the frenzied yapping of wild dogs, from the mopani thicket.

There was frost in the air and the small sounds near at hand sounded like the tinkling of ice. Tree-frogs kept up a monotonous tattoo that might have been the drumming of ghostly finger-nails on a window-pane. A host of unfamiliar insects made brittle, cold little sounds, as sharp as pin-pricks. Water wove a delicate pattern as it cascaded over a face of rock from its spring half-way up the koppie. And the stars had the icy brilliance of diamonds.

Even as Tom shivered, the roar boomed out once more, this time to the north.

Kameel changed his direction slightly, with Tom close behind him. The pace he set was so hard that the blood soon pounded warmly through Tom's body, and the cold was forgotten.

Tom was surprised at the direction taken by Kameel. It seemed to him to be off course from the direction the roar had indicated. But of course he followed closely, without comment. He knew he had everything to learn.

Suddenly Kameel froze in his tracks, and Tom did the same.

What had he seen, or heard? Tom could make out nothing even vaguely resembling an ostrich—or a lion!

Slowly the man raised his gun to his shoulder, hardly seeming to move at all. Then—*bang!* Even though he had been watching Kameel's every action, the report of the gun took Tom by surprise.

Then Kameel was running ahead, lightly and still silently. And Tom was shadowing him.

It was not until the hunter bent over

the dead body of the ostrich that Tom saw it. He had thought it to be a round boulder. But he could see now that the little wind ruffled the black and white feathers, and when Tom bent, as Kameel had done, and laid his hand on the body, it was soft and still warm.

Kameel squatted on the ground near the dead bird, and indicated that Tom should do the same. Until the first light of morning dimmed the stars they sat there, dozing or wakeful.

Then, expertly, Kameel skinned the bird. But first he plucked a lovely black plume from the ostrich's wing feathers and handed it to Tom. It was obviously a gift, and Tom accepted it with pleasure.

Suddenly, as he held the feather up against the sky the better to examine its perfection, he remembered a bonnet Aunt Polly had once worn with great pride in London. It was a black velvet bonnet with frills of white lace framing her face, and with black ostrich plumes for decoration which danced in every whisper of wind.

He could see her gaily pirouetting as she showed off her grand bonnet, her pink crinoline billowing out like an opening flower. And the way his mother had clapped her hands, and laughed.

Amethysts for Samantha and an ostrich plume for Aunt Polly. He was delighted with his riches.

'Oh, that's simple,' Chris said when Tom explained how Kameel had seemed to take a slightly different direction from that indicated by the ostrich's *brom*. 'These stupid birds never run straight, Tom. They always run a little in the round, and a little in the round, until they describe a circle. Hunters always cut across and meet the bird with this in mind.'

'They must be the world's strangest birds,' Tom declared. 'Who would expect a bird to roar like a lion and run in circles?'

'Hunters,' Chris laughed. 'We've got him sized up, I assure you, Tom.'

8

Gold Strike!

'Gold on the commonage? You must be joking, Sam!'

'There's no joke about it, Tom. You know Bernard Meintjes, the boy who lives two doors down the street?'

'Of course. Don't tell me he found it!'

'But he did. Oh, he wasn't looking for gold or anything like that. As a matter of fact he was looking for stones for his catapult, and he just happened to pick up this lump of gold.'

'When did it happen?'

'Only this morning. You've come home at the very height of the excitement. Oh, Tom, I have missed you. I'm so glad you and Chris have come back.'

'So am I, although the hunt was a grand experience. But what do you think will happen now, Sam? Will they start digging up the commonage? Good gracious—there may be gold under this house!'

'Well, of course. It could be anywhere. That's why everyone has gone quite mad about Bernard's find.'

'Not everyone, Samantha,' a quiet voice said behind them.

They wheeled round, almost guiltily.

'Oh, Mama! I think you—you and Oom Paul—are the only ones who aren't happy and excited about Bernard's strike.'

'But, Aunt Polly, you believe he did find the gold on the commonage, don't you?'

'Certainly, Tom. I have seen it. Unfortunately there can be no doubt about it.'

'Then—?'

'Pray why should gold make people mad? It does, I know, and that is the pity of it. But—oh, look at this village as it is now. Imagine what those men will do to it with their ruthless, senseless digging!'

There were tears in her eyes, which both Samantha and Tom could understand.

When Chris and Tom had ridden into Pretoria that afternoon after an absence of only three weeks, they had found that a transformation had taken place, even in that short time, following the first spring rains.

Pomegranate bushes were massed with scarlet lacquered buds and the gay explosions of their vivid blossoms, and in every garden there were snowy branches on apricot- and plum-trees, and gay pink banners of peach blossom. The few tight buds on the rose bushes which Samantha had pointed out with such pride a month ago, had given place to a glory of sweet-brier and pink monthly roses. The dry grass on the commonage and in Church Square had been burnt off just before the rains came, and green shoots were forcing their way through the short black stubble.

Tom had thought he had never seen a prettier sight in his life.

And now—would it all be wrecked as men dug for gold?

Bernard was the fourteen-year-old son of Stephanus Meintjes, the first Registrar of Deeds in the capital, a sober man in no way attracted to the Gold Rush that was introducing such complications to the Transvaal. How would he react to his son's find? Tom wondered. It was impossible to predict.

'If Mr. Kruger has his way no digging will be allowed on town lands. But can he enforce it when men have gone mad?' Mrs. Howes moved to the window and stood looking out across the commonage.

Groups of men were gathered there, and some women, all talking excitedly and studying the ground. One man had turned over several spadefuls of soil which he and his friends scooped up in their hands and minutely examined.

'You see, they have started already.' Mrs. Howes wrung her hands. 'Ah, your father and Christian have joined them, Samantha.'

Samantha and Tom were gone before she could stop them.

Chris appeared to be unmoved by the excitement of the others. In fact there was a coldness about him that Tom had not previously known. But Mr. Howes's reactions were very different.

'Papa has been longing to get away to Mac Mac ever since the first stories of lucky strikes began to come through to us,' Sam said. 'I wonder what he will do?

'If there's gold right here in Pretoria surely he won't want to leave now?'

Samantha shook her head. They had not joined the men, but stood at a little distance, eyes and ears alert.

'I'll tell you this, Tom. Most of the men I have listened to today believe Bernard's gold is something of a freak find. They don't think there's any rich deposit here. A little gold, yes. But not enough to cause a stampede. Of course they'll dig and find out for sure. But this sort of thing happens so often in South Africa. They've found gold at places all round Pretoria, but not rich deposits of the stuff.'

'What a gamble gold is!'

'Of course it is. That's why it drives people mad.' She paused, then said slowly, 'Shall I tell you something, Tom?'

'Mmm?'

'I feel a little of this madness myself. It's hard to explain, but I understand how Papa and those other men feel about it. It isn't that I want to be very rich or anything like that. It's just—well, it's just like playing an exciting game of hide-and-seek with Nature. A sort of challenge you want to go out and meet.'

'That's what Kangaroo Joe said.'

'Don't you feel it too?'

'I can't say I do. Mind you, I feel excited by this news of Bernard's find. And there's something—something about diggers that makes them seem, well, my sort of people, if you know what I mean, Sam. I'm in sympathy with them—I like them and the way they live.'

She nodded.

'Kangaroo Joe, and a man called Rollingstone Charlie we met on the hunt—they're different from ordinary people. Something seems to be burning them up inside.'

'Of course it does. Gold-fever.'

Chris saw them and came across to join them.

'Don't tell me you two are losing your senses too,' he laughed.

'What do you think about it, Chris? Do you think—?'

'I'll tell you what I think, Tom. This get-rich-quick thinking is no good to anyone. We're supposed to work for what we get.'

'You tell a digger he doesn't work,' Samantha suggested hotly.

'Tell a child it isn't working when it digs holes in a garden,' Chris retorted. 'These people are despoiling our land. What if they do strike a fortune? Many fortunes. It won't improve our country, will it? It will only scar it and leave the germs of unnatural fevers when the men have gone off with their gold.'

'Oh dear, you feel the same way about it that Mama and Oom Paul do.'

'Is that so bad? Most of us Boers feel like this, Samantha. Ah, well. By the signs this is nothing to worry about. Bernard Meintjes has found a little lump of gold. It has caused some excitement. A few holes will no doubt be dug on the commonage into which men will fall on their way home from that other "Hole—in the Wall". It has stirred up some madness. But that will pass.'

'You don't think they'll find more gold here?'

'Probably they will. But not very much—if those who say they know about such things are correct. In the past hour or so that I've spent here in Pretoria I have heard nothing—nothing at all—but *gold*! It sickens me. I am glad that I leave in the morning for my farm. There may be rocks of solid gold under the grass for all I care. What does matter is that the grass grows and life and work go on as usual. We Boers may be dull people, but at least we're content to be pastural.'

'Why do you always forget that you are only half Boer, Chris?' Samantha demanded. 'Doesn't that English half of you count for anything?'

He laughed shortly. 'It counts for much. But, thank God, there is no gold-fever in my English blood, Sam.'

'Look who's here!' Tom cried.

A tall, thin man approached them, and at sight of him Chris gave a shout of welcome and went to meet him with hand outstretched.

'So you have got here at last, Meneer Williams,' he said, shaking hands. 'Man, but it's good to see you again.'

'Believe me, it's good to be here. Even a year in the country hasn't conditioned me to the pace of an ox, and my wife is weary of travelling. Ah, Tom, I would hardly have known you, you're so brown and tough. I have your kudu horns in the wagon. Christian said they were to be kept for you.'

'Oh thanks! Mr. Williams, this is my cousin, Samantha. We spent a night with him on the hunt, Sam.'

Mr. Howes joined them and was introduced.

'And where is your wagon?' he asked.

'I have outspanned in Town Square, not far from here.'

'Then I suggest we go along now and see if there is any way in which we can help to make you comfortable. You and your family will take pot luck with us this evening, I hope. It will give my wife such pleasure to have someone from the Old Country to talk to.'

Samantha slipped home to prepare her mother, and help with the evening meal.

There was a storm that evening and one of the children was running a slight temperature, so Mrs. Howes insisted that the whole family stay the night with them. She was, as her husband had said, delighted to have Mrs. Williams for company. They had much in common.

'You won't mind sleeping on the sofa, will you, Christian?'

'That will suit me very well, Mevrou Howes.'

'We have a large spare room and plenty of beds. Do please stay, Mrs. Williams.'

There was no need for the two women to explain to one another all the homesickness and loneliness they had endured in this strange land. It was all too obvious.

And it came as no real surprise when the Williams family were persuaded to remain on as guests the following day.

'I am deeply grateful for all you have done for Tom,' Mr. Howes told Chris as he prepared to leave the next morning. 'You have made a man of him.'

'Oh, I take no credit for that,' Chris said, smiling. 'Tom was a man in the making before I came along. He has grown up overnight, that's all. I've enjoyed his company.'

Mr. Williams had not only given Tom his prized kudu horns, but a strip of the skin of his first 'kill' to adorn his hat, as was the custom.

'I've a feeling that won't be our last hunt together, Tom,' Chris said, before riding off. 'I would like you to come out to the farm and see how we tan the skins with acacia bark, and make the giraffe-skin whips and hippo-hide sjamboks. And perhaps next year you will make the trip to the coast with me. I'd like that.'

'So would I, Chris. Thanks—for everything.'

Samantha's eyes danced with mischief.

'I may not be a gipsy fortune-teller, but I foresee something very different in store for you, Chris le Roux.'

'You do, do you?'

'I foresee you going down with gold-fever, and forsaking the game trail for the diggings.'

Chris laughed and pressed his heels into his horse's sides.

'If that should happen I'll give you my first lucky strike, Sam! But don't rely on it, or you'll die a pauper.'

*

The usually placid life of the capital had been badly disrupted by Bernard's find. The sound of digging, and of men's voices raised in argument and excited discussion, destroyed the peace. More gold was found, to add zest to the search, although in small quantities.

Mrs. Howes was glad to have Mrs. Williams's company, and the distraction of helping to care for the children.

But there were other rude shocks in store for her.

The first was unwittingly inflicted by Mr. Williams, who had the highest regard for President Burgers and his progressive ideas.

'I have just heard a remarkable story about the President,' he said as they sat drinking coffee round the fire one evening. His eyes were on his wife so that he missed the signal Mr. Howes tried to give him, and went on with enthusiasm: 'It concerns a Coloured man convicted of murder, who was due to be hanged in the morning. The President has immediately arranged a pardon for the man and taken him into his employment. It seems he is a wizard with roses. In fact he was taught the art of rose culture in the Cape where he worked before being brought to the Transvaal by a builder named de Villiers, who intended to use the man's skill in laying out rose gardens here in the capital.'

'Do you mean,' Mrs. Howes said in a shocked voice, her face drained of all colour, 'do you mean President Burgers has pardoned a murderer—let the man loose in our midst—so that his roses—?'

'My dear,' her husband said quickly, placing a hand on her arm, 'do not distress yourself. It isn't as bad as that sounds, I'm quite sure.'

'But those are the facts, aren't they?' she demanded.

'Well, yes, they are.' Mr. Williams was taken aback by her reaction to his piece of local news. 'But the man isn't a desperate character I am quite sure.'

'What makes you so sure, Mr. Williams? He has taken a life. No doubt he could take others—given the opportunity.'

'There are very different kinds of murder, my dear,' her husband reasoned. 'Some good men have killed in self-defence, or when defending others, for instance.'

'I prefer to remember the Law, "Thou shalt not kill". What kind of example is the President setting by condoning murder?

And for the sake of his rose garden! Had this man not understood the care of roses would the President have had him pardoned—or would he have hanged?'

'Polly, we know the kind of man President Burgers is. His goodness and tolerance are beyond question. He was a man of God before he saw politics as his field of work. Shouldn't we withhold judgement until all the facts are known to us?'

'You men see things differently from us women.' There were tears in her eyes. She turned to Mrs. Williams for support, but saw at once that she felt as her husband did in this matter. 'You feel the same way?' she faltered.

'My dear, you distress yourself without knowing all the facts, as your husband says,' Mrs. Williams said gently.

Polly Howes stood up, anger drying the tears from her eyes. Her knuckles were white as she clenched the back of her chair.

'The facts I do know are enough for me!' she cried. 'We are a few civilized people living in a savage land. The only hope for our survival lies in maintaining our standards. In setting an example these people will recognize and come to respect. And here is our President—condoning murder—for his own paltry, selfish ends. I am sorry, you must excuse me. This—this—and your attitude—all of you—!' She ran from the room, and her bedroom door closed with a bang.

'I'm so very sorry,' Mr. Williams apologized to his host. 'I had no idea Mrs. Howes would feel this way—'

'How could you know? This country terrifies my wife, and the Natives no less. Her dislike of everything here arises from fear. You will excuse me? I must go to her. Please try not to be distressed by what has happened. It will pass.'

But although Mrs. Howes apologized to her guests the following morning, the happy atmosphere had gone.

At midday Mr. Williams returned from the village in a state of excitement. He was a straight-speaking man, and chose to ignore the tension that existed.

'I have just come from President Burgers,' he said without preamble. 'I thought it best to find out the facts directly from him, and he explained matters to me freely. It seems that this man did indeed kill in self-defence, and was known to the President before the incident. He vouches for the man's character.'

He smiled at Mrs. Howes. 'Will you accept that—from a man whose honour has never been questioned even by his enemies?'

'Very well. I will accept his explanation,' Mrs. Howes agreed after a moment's hesitation. However, she gave no answering smile.

'I'm glad of that. But there is something more!' Mr. Williams went to his wife and cupped her shoulders in his hands, giving her a little shake in his excitement. 'Oh, Clare, I have such good news for you, my dear!' he said.

'Yes, Harry?'

'Our days of wandering are over. We can stay in this delightful place. The President has offered me the post of schoolmaster here in Pretoria. I am to open the first school in the capital—immediately.'

Only Polly Howes understood the courage it took for her friend to lift her chin and return her husband's smile. Only she knew how much Clare Williams had longed to return to her relatives and friends and her old way of life across the sea. She was bidding them all farewell in her heart, and the two women knew it.

'You have accepted the offer?' she asked.

'Yes, my dear, I have.'

'Then that is wonderful news. I am so happy for you, believe me!'

'And for you, and the children,' he went on. 'It will mean settling in a home among friendly people, and I will be doing my kind of work again. Clare, you are sure this is what you want?'

'Of course—quite sure,' she smiled.

Nor was that all that happened on that momentous day.

Out of sight of his home, Mr. Howes had been digging alongside the other men, with Tom sifting the soil as he turned it.

Once or twice a shout had gone up as a lucky digger had found a trace of gold—nothing more. No nuggets had been found that day. If the findings warranted it, serious work would begin very soon, but now they were exploring the possibilities with much pick and shovel work, and even more discussion and argument.

The light was failing when Andrew Howes made his lucky strike. Certainly it was a much smaller nugget than Bernard

Meintjes had found—but gold it was. The men who gathered round to inspect his find, some of whom were experienced diggers, had no doubt about it. The important part it was to play in the lives of the Howes family, and of Tom, was out of all proportion to its size.

This was the sign Andrew Howes had been waiting for. He had dug for gold—and he had found it. There could be no turning back now. The fever was in his blood.

'We are going to Mac Mac,' he told his wife, holding up the prize that left her cold.

It was only the memory of the brave way in which Mrs. Williams had accepted her husband's decision earlier that day, that gave Mrs. Howes the courage to stand up to the blow.

'And if that fails?' she asked quietly.

'Then we will return to England, Polly. It is impossible for us to remain here, as you know. There is no work for me in Pretoria. And you found D'Urban and Pietermaritzburg unbearable. I ask you to stand by me while we try our fortunes at Mac Mac, and I promise you that if that fails we will waste no more time in this country, but will return—home. You will do this for me?'

'Yes, Andrew. We will go to Mac Mac,' his wife said steadily.

Tom was chopping wood the next morning and Samantha was neatly stacking it.

'Have you ever known anything like it, Tom?' Sam said. 'Suddenly *everything* is happening. The world is on its head. Oh, I can't tell you how happy I am!'

'It's what you want, isn't it? You have no fears, Sam?'

She straightened up and laughed at the very idea.

'Fears? I'm as delighted about it as Papa is. I feel as though this is what we've been waiting for.'

'You know, Sam, if we were to tell people in England that your father has just bartered his furnished house for an ox-wagon and team, they would never believe it.'

'Probably not. But it makes good sense to us, doesn't it? We need the wagon for our trek to Mac Mac, and Mr. Williams needs our house here in Pretoria. Neither Papa nor Mr. Williams has much money, so they couldn't have bought them. Barter's the only way we can manage things here, and it's so simple, isn't it?'

'I'm glad we can take our horses. I would have hated to lose Star,' Tom said presently, making the splinters fly with his axe.

Samantha sighed. 'Yes, I'm glad about it too. But we have to be prepared for the fact that they'll probably die.'

'Sam! You don't mean that!' Tom stared at her in shocked amazement.

'Well, of course. I'd just as soon leave Diamond here. You know neither of our horses is salted. We're taking them down into fever country.'

'How can you be so—so casual about it?' Tom exclaimed. 'Don't you love your horse?'

'You know I do! But I thought about it for hours and hours last night in bed, Tom. If I left Diamond here how would I know she'd be properly cared for? And, anyway, she could be killed by a lion or a leopard, couldn't she? It is just possible that neither Diamond or Star will get fever. They stand about the same chance of survival whether we leave them here or take them along with us. So we'll take them along.'

Tom sighed and rubbed the palms of his hands together before resuming his chopping.

'You know, Sam,' he said presently, 'you look at these things the same way that Chris does. You're philosophical, even about death.'

Samantha smiled at him.

'I think one learns to be in this country. There's so much death here, isn't there? Not like in England, where only fowls were killed for the pot, and a turkey at Christmas. But Chris and I aren't really alike, you know. I love South Africa, but not the way he does. The Boer way. Mind you, in time I may learn to.'

'I shouldn't wonder if you do, Sam. Ah, that's the lot, thank goodness.'

9
TREK!

Now that the decision had been taken to seek his fortune at the diggings, Andrew Howes was anxious to be on his way.

Preparations for the long journey kept the family busy every waking hour. They were to take only what they would need, he stressed, and all other possessions must be packed away in tin trunks and stored in the ceiling of the house that would no longer be their home.

'I suppose it is foolish to keep my London clothes,' Mrs. Howes said wistfully. 'After all, if ever I do have an opportunity to wear them again they will be out of fashion. But my lavender silk gown I refuse to leave behind. Even though I am able to do no more than take it out and look at it occasionally, it will bring back happy memories and give me pleasure.'

And so she carefully packed away the lavender silk crinoline in scented tissue paper, and with it the taffeta petticoats, beribboned bonnet, mittens and parasol. A treasured bottle of French perfume and an exquisite painted silk fan were included, with a pair of matching silk slippers.

The large trunk was packed into the wagon box under the driver's seat, and although it took up valuable space which should have been used for such necessities as bedding and working clothes, nothing was said about it.

Fortunately the wagon was well fitted and ready for the road. Sacks of meal and many boxes of tinned provisions, tents, tools and ammunition, were bought and stored on the floor of the wagon, over which the big litter bed fitted like a lid. It was quite light, being merely a strong, reinforced wooden frame with a close criss-cross of hide riems which formed the mattress. Soft skins, cushions, and many blankets and quilts were piled on the bed, and it was usual for an entire family to sleep there by night, and to rest at times during the day. A heavy dust sheet was spread over all while the wagon was on the move.

No space was wasted. The barrels were filled with fresh water and safely stored. The three-legged cooking-pots, frying-pan, pails and benches, were hung on hooks under the wagon. And a large chicken-coop was strapped to the high wooden step. No traveller would dream of setting out on a journey by ox-wagon without one or more cocks to serve the important role of alarum-clock. The day's trek had to start before sunrise, and the first cock-crow was literally their signal that another day had begun.

One of their greatest strokes of good fortune, as it was to prove, was the engaging of a Zulu driver named Mutwa.

He had just done the trip up from D'Urban with a family named Robinson, who were settling in Pretoria, and they strongly urged Mr. Howes to employ Mutwa as he was prepared to do the journey to Mac Mac, and was evidently in no haste to return home to Natal.

'We could never have managed without him,' Mr. Robinson declared. 'He was taken on as a driver, but believe me there is nothing he can't do. We have become attached to him and are sorry to see him go. Apart from all else, he's an excellent camp cook, and he speaks English.'

Although Mrs. Howes was most reluctant to agree to Mutwa's engagement, she came to realize that her husband would need practical assistance on the very difficult journey that faced them.

'You need have no contact with the man, my dear,' Andrew Howes had reasoned when at first she objected. 'As you know, I have had no experience whatever of driving a team of oxen, and they tell me the mountain passes are perilous. It would be madness for us to attempt the journey without a thoroughly experienced driver.'

The packing of the wagon alone was a test of skilled workmanship, and, from the outset, Mutwa proved to be invaluable.

Every item had to be neatly packed away, and easily available when needed. Nothing must rattle or be in danger of swinging loose on rough or precipitous roads, and the oxen demanded special understanding and handling. All of this, and much more, Mutwa attended to with the ease of much experience.

The Zulus were a nation of warriors, and Mutwa had the splendid physique and quick intelligence common to his people.

The Howes' leave-taking was an emotional ordeal, for a large crowd of friends and well-wishers gathered to bid them God-speed and good fortune.

Every day more men were leaving for Mac Mac, and those who could not get away were openly envious, renewing their efforts to cut their ties with Pretoria and be on their way to what they believed would be certain fortune.

Mrs. Howes surprised her family, who had been prepared for tears. Some of her old spirit had returned to her in the past few trying days, and she smiled and sang out her farewells as though she were leaving without regrets or fears. Only when she and Mrs. Williams embraced for the last time did she show emotion, but this was quickly hidden.

'Anything is better than the dead and alive existence we have been living here in Pretoria,' she had confided to her friend the day before. 'At least we will be moving towards a new life—whether it proves to be one of fortune, or our return to England.'

Mutwa hooked the canvas water bag on the peg in front of the wagon, where evaporation in the sun would keep the contents cool. He went to the head of the team and picked up the leading riem, pulling the front oxen round in a semi-circle so that the trek chain that linked them was loosened and lay in position on the back of each beast. Then he called Tom and handed the leading riem over to him, for it had been decided that Tom would voorloop for a while.

Samantha swung up into her saddle, leading Star, and walked the horses to join Tom.

At last everything was ready for the journey. Mr. Howes helped his wife up onto the high driver's seat, and Mutwa took his place beside him, picking up the reins and shaking the long whip loose.

'All right, Mutwa, we go,' Andrew Howes said quietly.

The whip cracked in the air over the backs of the oxen. '*Tou!*' Mutwa shouted on a high, nasal note. Couple by couple the oxen took the strain, leaning forward in the yoke, and the heavy wagon rumbled off amid the shouts and good wishes of friends.

Polly Howes turned for one last look at the house that had been their home. Already it was taking on a new appearance and was vaguely unfamiliar. Children's clothes filled the lines in the back yard, doors and windows were thrown wide as she had never permitted them to be because of the dust from passing wagons. And Mrs. Williams stood on the top step, a child in her arms, waving a last good-bye.

Once clear of the town and out on the rough wagon road, Mutwa secured the reins and slipped the whip back into its socket.

'I go to voorloop,' he said, smiling. 'The oxen have found their legs, baas. No need to drive, they go now.'

He jumped down while the wagon creaked slowly on its way, and relieved Tom at the head of the team. And Tom was only too glad to mount Star and ride ahead with Sam. The exciting challenge of the open road was gripping them all in various ways, and it seemed a good omen that their adventure had begun on such a perfect day.

The air was heavy with the honey-sweet fragrance of mimosa and white-flowering buffelpeer, and the camelthorn trees were bright with spring foliage.

Lydenburg was a good twelve days' trek from Pretoria, and Mac Mac a few days' perilous mountain travel farther on.

Almost at once they settled down into a state of timelessness, such as one knows at sea. Every day was the same routine of the pre-dawn start, and an outspan every two hours for the oxen to rest and graze. Each of these short treks was called a skof, and the length of the day's journey was reckoned by the number of skofs.

Because the oxen travelled at three miles an hour at most, Samantha and Tom could enjoy rides or walks in the veld and always be sure of catching up with the wagon. Unless rain had recently fallen, a trail of dust in the air signalled its whereabouts, for the tracks were faint.

Quite soon Mrs. Howes forgot that she had ever been afraid of Mutwa, and accepted him as naturally as the others did. He showed her how to cook scones and mealie bread, and tasty stews, over the camp fire. She would wander over the veld gathering mushrooms after rain, and for the first time something of the beauty and magic of the veld got through to her, and she realized that she had not really seen the countryside until now. On their first journey up from the coast her fear and misery had made her blind to the passing scene. Everything had frightened her and she had shrunk from the vastness of the veld, the mountains and the sky, longing only for London.

Mr. Howes, Sam and Tom were taught by Mutwa how to handle the oxen and drive the wagon, and they also shot for the pot. Now and then Sam would climb up on top of the tent sail to get a wider view, and she loved to sit up there alone, singing to herself and watching the wild life all about them.

During the heat of the day they always outspanned and slept the hot hours away. And evenings round the camp fire were the perfect end to each full day.

For the first hundred miles they passed through open, undulating country, occasionally meeting up with other travellers going to or coming from the diggings, and exchanging news. It was always a great event when another wagon, horseman, or digger plodding alongside his laden mule, came in sight.

And it was only then that the talk turned to the diggings. Otherwise gold was pushed out of mind by the hourly happenings of the timeless journey. They seemed to have forgotten what lay behind, and not to care what lay ahead of them. All of life seemed to consist of the day's travel.

One morning Samantha was riding on the driver's seat with her mother, enjoying the sun on her face and the swaying motion of the wagon, when she noticed the strange way a small grey bird with a reddish beak was behaving. It was the size of a sparrow, and it flew alongside the wagon, making a shrill hissing cry, and sometimes almost flying into their faces.

'Whatever is the matter with this bird?' Mrs. Howes exclaimed, warding it off with upraised arm. 'It seems to be attacking us!'

'Mutwa!' Sam called. 'Look at this bird. We can't drive it off.'

'Do not try to!' Mutwa cried in alarm. 'That is the honey-bird, N'kosana. It wants to show us where the honey is. If you harm that bird great bad things will happen to you. When we outspan just now we will let him take us to the honey.'

The bird stayed with them until a halt was called, and as soon as they had outspanned, Mutwa, Samantha and Tom set off to follow it, carrying buckets, spades and hatchets.

The bird had flown to a neighbouring tree, and as they approached, it flitted to the next, and then on to the next tree when they came up with it, leading them on. When the way was rough or steep and they couldn't catch up with it, the bird flew back, uttering shrill cries of impatience. When no tree was at hand for it to settle on, it flew in circles in the air until they caught up.

For nearly a mile it led them over a difficult path through bush and over rocks. And at last it stopped in a small clump of mimosa trees. It flew from one to another of the trees in great excitement. Mutwa examined the trunks but could find no sign of a hive. The bird grew more angry than ever, and with piercing cries settled on the trunk of one of the trees before which it had been flitting back and forth.

Only then did they see what the bird was trying to show them! A small hole surrounded by a kind of cement. While they watched, a bee flew into the hole. Another followed it.

'There will be much honey,' Mutwa said, delighted. 'We must have dry grass.'

Taking a large handful of the dry grass they soon gathered, Mutwa lit it and then struck the mouth of the narrow hole with the hatchet. At the first blow a quantity of mud, wax and decayed wood fell to the ground, with which the wild bees had skilfully walled up a large portion of the decaying trunk.

Out swarmed a cloud of bees, and now the burning grass came into operation. As quickly as they flew out their wings were singed in the flames or the smoke dazed them, and they fell to the ground.

With a little cutting a large portion of the combs was exposed. They were laid horizontally across the entire width of the hollow trunk, and three buckets were filled with the dripping honeycomb, while they had to leave twice that amount untouched.

Before leaving, Mutwa hung a large piece of honeycomb on a thornbush for the guide-bird, and for a few minutes they watched while it began its feast.

'You must always leave some honey for the bird, or big trouble will come to you,' Mutwa explained.

'But how did it know we would understand it?' Samantha puzzled. 'And if we hadn't come along, who would have broken the hive open for it?'

Mutwa laughed and shook his head, munching a mouthful of honeycomb. All his life he had been used to the strange ways of the guide-bird. One accepted it along with the many good things of life, like sunshine, rain, and a full stomach. One asked no questions.

10

The Killer

The trek ceased to be a picnic and became a nightmare when the plains were left behind and they took to the mountains. Here the rough track snaked up seemingly impossible gradients, skirted precipices, and plunged into deep valleys.

The oxen sweated and laboured, and everyone became hoarse from shouting to urge them on. Often the whip was brought down across the beasts' straining backs to avert the disaster of their coming to a standstill on a steep mountain-side, when it would have been almost impossible to get the wagon moving again, if, indeed, they managed to prevent it from overturning or rolling into the valley below.

Mrs. Howes could not bear to see the oxen thrashed, and so she and Samantha would take another route or remain behind until the horror was past.

They only stopped at the pretty hamlet of Lydenburg long enough for the luxury of hot baths at the new hotel, and to purchase necessary stores. Then they pressed on.

Negotiating the Steenkamp mountains had been bad enough, but they knew that much worse lay between Lydenburg and Mac Mac. Not only was the track precipitous and extremely dangerous, and the toll of serious accidents frightening, but they were in the heavy mist belt, and all too often an ocean of mist rolled up from the Lowveld, blanketing out the world and making travel impossible.

Over the dreadful Devil's Knuckles they struggled, and up the endless Long Tom Pass, rising to 7,000 feet. They would never have done it had Mutwa not taken charge, and even he had long since ceased to sing and smile as he faced the dangers they had constantly to meet and overcome.

When at last they reached a small plateau on the slopes of the Mauchberg one afternoon, they were only too glad to call a halt and pitch camp.

'With luck we should reach Mac Mac tomorrow afternoon, if we strike a clear morning,' Mr. Howes tried to cheer his wife. 'It will be the end of our journey, and the start of a new life, dear Polly. The mist's coming up. I'll just have time to shoot something for the pot before everything is blotted out again.'

'Don't go far, dear. Don't go far!' his wife pleaded.

'I shan't, I promise you. Don't worry, Polly.'

Tom saw the tension in his aunt's face, and said quickly:

'Let me go, Uncle Andrew. I've my rifle here, and I can ride Diamond. She's saddled, and Sam won't mind.'

'Right. Thanks, Tom. Mutwa needs help here anyway.'

Tom only just beat the mist on his return. A small buck was slung over the front of his saddle, and he lowered this to the ground before dismounting.

A big fire was burning, tended by Mrs. Howes and Samantha. Mutwa was still busy with the oxen. They would have to remain within the circle of firelight during the night.

'We'll tether the horses under this big tree,' Mr. Howes said. 'Mutwa has almost finished with the oxen and he'll get the meat ready for the pot. Here, give me the reins, Tom. I'll attend to Diamond while you fetch Star.'

What happened in the next few minutes would remain to haunt them all their lives.

As Mr. Howes unsaddled Diamond under the wide-spreading tree, there was suddenly a ferocious growl from the branch overhead, and a leopard sprang upon the horse, bringing it to the ground, and sinking its fangs into Diamond's neck.

A sjambok, which they had used on the oxen during the last difficult haul, lay on the ground near by. Andrew Howes snatched it up and brought it down with a crack across the leopard's back.

Like a fury the leopard turned on him, pinning him under its great weight, and savaging his leg.

'Keep clear!' Tom yelled to Samantha as she was about to rush to her father's aid.

Raising his gun, Tom waited for the split second when he could fire without endangering his uncle's life. Then the gun roared, and the terrible struggle on the ground was over. The leopard lay dead across the unconscious body of the man.

It was necessary for Tom to fire again to put Diamond out of her agony.

Mutwa had to restrain and quieten the oxen to prevent a stampede. Then he joined the others who were doing all they could for Andrew Howes.

Tom had run to the wagon for the chest which contained their basic medical and surgical needs.

After the first paralysing moment of anguish, his aunt had suddenly become strong and calm and had actually taken command of the situation, with no sign of her usual nervousness.

'Fetch a kaross, Samantha, and blankets,' she directed. 'Spread them near the fire. Then light all the lanterns you can find. Tom, you and Mutwa must carry Andrew to the fire—the light.'

There was a large pot of boiling water on the fire and everyone did what they could without panic.

The wounds were serious, and it took all Polly Howes's new-found reserves of courage and self-control to clean and dress them as well as she could, and to staunch the flow of blood.

During this operation her husband regained consciousness.

'We have nothing—nothing whatever to relieve your pain,' his wife told him. 'Oh, Andrew, my dear!'

'I can stand it, Polly.'

'There's a farm-house not far from here—not more than a couple of miles at most,' Tom said. 'I saw it when I was getting the buck. Shall I go for help?'

'In this mist? You would be killed—or lose your way. Wait until there's some—light,' his uncle whispered.

Mutwa squatted on the ground beside the wounded man.

'Baas—I mix herb drink. Make you sleep. You will take it?'

For a moment they looked at each other steadily. Then Andrew Howes nodded and closed his eyes, and Mutwa went to work quickly.

Tom had wondered what was contained in the several tiny antelope horns, with their bark stoppers, which Mutwa wore threaded on a fine leather throng round his neck. He had guessed that it was snuff. Now he saw the man carefully measure finely powdered herbs from one of the horns into a mug, which he mixed with boiling water, stirring it until it was cool enough to drink.

'This good. Baas will sleep,' Mutwa told Polly Howes, seeing the doubt and fear in her eyes.

Kneeling beside the wounded man he gently raised his head and held the mug to his lips. The three who watched held their breath. Very soon after Mutwa had lowered his head to the cushion, the tension in Andrew Howes's face and body eased. He began to breathe more deeply and easily. Once he opened his eyes a little and smiled faintly into his wife's anxious face as she bent over him.

Then he slept.

'Oh, thank you, Mutwa! But it will do no harm? When he wakes—?'

'This is good medicine. My people use it. You will see,' the man promised.

Samantha made coffee while her mother remained watching the sleeping man. Then, expertly, Mutwa showed Tom how to make a stretcher, using two tent poles, and lashing skins across it which were then padded with a blanket.

Towards midnight the wind changed direction, blowing lightly but steadily from the north and sweeping the mist before it. The sky was almost clear, and moonlight flooded the world.

'I'm going for help, Aunt Polly,' Tom told her. 'The farm-house I saw isn't far from here. We'll be back in no time.'

'We?'

'I'm riding Star. It will be quicker and safer. The wind may turn again at any time and bring the mist back. Mutwa will be here with you and Sam.'

As he saddled his horse he asked Mutwa, 'You can shoot?'

Mutwa nodded.

'Then fetch my uncle's gun from the wagon. Keep it by you, Mutwa. You may need it.'

When Tom dismounted at the farm-house and looped his reins over the hitching post, a wild chorus of barking broke out from the fenced back yard.

A window was thrown open and a man's head appeared.

'Who is there?' he demanded in a gruff voice. He spoke Dutch, and Tom's heart sank.

'Forgive the hour, Meneer,' Tom shouted back above the barking. 'A leopard has wounded my uncle, and we need help.'

'Magtig!' the man grunted, withdrawing his head.

A lamp was lit in the room and presently the front door was unlatched. Tom could hear two voices, a man's and a woman's, talking, and then the man appeared at the door, a lamp held high so that he could see his midnight visitor.

Tom thought the farmer must surely be the largest man he had ever seen. He filled the doorway. His tousled hair and flowing beard were grey, and he had hastily pulled on his corduroys and was trying to tuck in his shirt with his free hand.

'Someone is hurt, you say?' he said.

Tom sighed with relief. The man spoke English. The sooner he learned Dutch the better, but he was reluctant to try out the few words he knew for fear of ridicule.

'My uncle. We are outspanned about two miles from here, meneer. The leopard attacked the horse, and then my uncle when he struck it.'

'That must be the brute I've been after. It is a killer,' the man said, and turned to make an excited remark to his wife. 'It never runs—it attacks. And it killed one of my boys not long ago. You got it?'

Tom nodded. 'Yes, it's dead,' he said. 'But my uncle—'

'I will come at once.'

The man stepped back and Tom saw the small woman who had been hidden by his great frame. She smiled at Tom, as she and her husband again conferred in their own language.

Suddenly all was commotion and activity. The man stalked to the back door, opened it and bellowed, '*Klaas! Japie! Katie!*' And at once there were answering shouts.

'What is your name?' his wife asked in careful English.

'Tom Maxwell. We are on our way to Mac Mac.'

She nodded. 'Our name is Viljoen. All will be ready when you return.'

Three figures came hurrying from across the yard, and Meneer Viljoen gave them directions that sent the two men scurrying across to a shed, while the fat old Native woman entered the back door tying on her apron and then tugging her doek straight on her head.

Andrew Howes still slept when they reached camp. Tom rode ahead of the light wagon drawn by a team of four mules, and the farmer had brought his two Natives with him to help.

From the moment the big man climbed down from the wagon and strode across to take Polly Howes's hand in his firm grasp, he gave them comfort and confidence. After a brief conversation in Zulu with Mutwa, he smiled his reassurance.

'The herbs he gave your husband are what we Boers always use in such cases. Most of our medicines come from the veld, and you can be sure that this is very good. I think your man should sleep until we get him to the farm. My vrou will be ready. You need not fear. She has had much experience with sickness and tending wounds.'

'Oh, thank you,' Polly Howes said through dry lips, watching as they carefully placed her husband on the stretcher and carried him to the light wagon. She had seen his wounds and knew how serious they were.

'My boys will stay here to help break camp and bring your

wagon and things down to the farm,' Meneer Viljoen said as he helped Mrs. Howes and Samantha up into his wagon. 'We will travel slowly so that he is not jolted too roughly. We will soon be there.'

Although Andrew Howes moaned whenever the wagon lurched, he did not waken. His wife held his hand tightly in hers, and her eyes never left his face.

Lights burned in all the rooms at the farm-house, and Anna Viljoen came onto the stoep to meet them, a lamp in her hand.

'The room is ready,' she said as the stretcher was carried indoors. She placed a hand on Polly Howes's arm. 'We will do all we can to help you, be sure of that, Mevrou,' she said.

Boiling water, clean dressings, and the usual farm medicine chest were at hand in the bedroom.

Cocks were crowing when at last Mevrou Viljoen had dressed the wounds and made Andrew Howes comfortable. They had given him more herbs to drink when he became restless, and again he slept.

She met Polly's eyes across the bed, and she smiled and nodded.

'Your man will live. Have no fear. He will not even lose his leg, and his other wounds will heal in time. He is very lucky, Mevrou Howes.'

'You have been wonderful!'

'But no. I have tended many wounded men. You will eat and you will sleep, while I watch here. Food is ready.'

'Oh, no, I couldn't—'

'But you will,' Anna Viljoen said firmly. 'Your man will need your strength to lean on. We women dare not be weak, Mevrou.'

Looking into those steady blue eyes, Polly Howes knew that she was right. In this untamed land a woman must be strong.

11

The Price of a Farm

It was soon clear that, while Andrew Howes's wounds were slowly healing without complications setting in, his convalescence would be a long one. His back had been badly hurt during his struggle against the leopard, and this gave him pain and discomfort.

'Man, it is good to have someone to talk to,' Dan Viljoen told him when he expressed his concern at the demands he and his family were making on the farmer's hospitality. 'Believe me, I have many problems and it helps a man to talk about them.'

And, gradually, he brought his problems into the open and discussed them with Andrew Howes, just as his wife talked about hers with Polly.

'Why did they have to find gold in my part of the country?' he demanded, looking like an enraged and sorrowing prophet with his great physique and long grey beard. 'All was peaceful here before they came. This is a good farm, and I could have made it into one of the best.'

'No doubt you will yet, Dan, in spite of the Gold Rush.'

'Never! We are beaten, and we know it. My farm is for sale. But who will buy it, tell me that?'

'How can these diggers have ruined your farm? I would have expected them to provide you with a market for your produce, not pose a threat to your existence.'

'That is because you have not seen these men. Nor do you know the things they do. They are madmen. They destroy the handiwork of the Lord—and they destroy one another.

'Listen to these things, my friend, and judge for yourself. A party of men led by Herbert Rhodes brought a wagonload of liquor to Mac Mac and opened a den of iniquity called "The Spotted Dog," where the diggers drink and brawl. More than that. He and his friends are gun-running. Selling firearms to the Kaffirs. We will have war here without any doubt. They are building it up. I hear Rhodes has even promised to supply the

Bapedi chief Secucuni with a canon—to be used against the white man!'

'This man, Herbert Rhodes. He is surely not related to Cecil Rhodes of Kimberley?'

'His brother, and a rogue. These diggers are men without honour. They would do anything for gold.' Suddenly he laughed, a short, hard burst of sound, without humour. 'Oh, I know you are on your way to the diggings, my friend,' he said. 'But make no mistake—you are no digger. I know these men. They are all kinds from all lands. But you are not one of them.'

'Nevertheless—' Andrew Howes prepared to argue.

'Oh, I know, man, I know. You too want gold. Perhaps you will find some. Who can tell? But you will find that the price is too high. Your vrou—your child—the boy. When you are strong again you must go to Mac Mac and see for yourself. And you will know in time that I am right.'

'Maybe so. We shall see. Each man must find out for himself, Dan. But if you sell your farm where will you go?'

'We are going to my brother's farm near Potchefstroom. It is good for a family to close in together when danger threatens.'

'Then you really do think there will be another war?'

'Of course. There can be no doubt. There are many signs.'

'I can only pray that you are wrong, my friend.'

Again and again in the long, peaceful days of convalescence, Dan Viljoen's talk returned to the possibility of war, and to the iniquities of the diggers.

'They are godless men,' he declared one day. 'They have no respect for the Will of Almighty God. I have only been to Mac Mac once since this insane Gold Rush began, and what I saw—it was terrible, I tell you man, terrible!

'That beautiful river they are tearing apart—looking for gold under the rocks that have formed its natural bed for centuries. One of these madmen even blasted the great rock at the top of the Mac Mac Falls, so that for all time the water which one flowed in a single sheet from that great height, will form two Falls, not one, as God intended.'

'He blasted with dynamite?'

Dan Viljoen nodded.

'Fortunately he blew himself up as well. So there is one fool less to tamper with Nature,' he said with satisfaction. 'Until I shot one of them in the leg for trespassing, and word got around, I was plagued by these men. They think there is gold under my land. And they want it. More than that, they want to change the course of the river that flows through my lands—to change the course God meant it to take. It is blasphemous! I told them I would shoot the next man who came to worry me—and not to wound, Andries. Not to wound next time.'

Good heavens, he meant it! Andrew Howes thought with shock. And marvelled that a man so kind to strangers under his roof, could yet be so hard.

Samantha and Tom took a lively interest in everything to do with the running of the farm, even though they fretted to be off to Mac Mac now that Andrew Howes was out of danger.

Strips of biltong were hanging to dry in the shade of the trees near the farm-house. Many skins were stretched and pegged down in the yard, being treated for the D'Urban market. Fowls ran in a large enclosed run, protected from wild animals, hawks and eagles. In a shed at the back skins, ivory and horns were stacked, ready for sale.

And in the big kitchen Tante Anna and Katie were constantly busy. They showed Mrs. Howes and Samantha how to make Boer bread and all kinds of biscuits, preserves and boerewors.

'We will leave here soon,' Anna Viljoen explained one morning to her new friend. 'Things will be safer and easier back at the old farm, but I will miss much that we have known here. And I think I will always regret that I have not been able to do the things I want to do.'

'What kind of things, Anna?'

'Although I would never confess it to him, I do not feel as strongly as my man does about the diggers.' She had lowered her voice. 'Those men need the vegetables we grow, and the good things Katie and I bake in this kitchen. They are hungry men and we could feed them.'

'They would pay you?'

'Oh, yes. Perhaps with raw gold. But they would pay.'

'Oh, Anna, I am so sorry.'

Anna Viljoen laughed merrily.

'For what? That I cannot have all the things I want? I do not expect them, Polly. Life has taught me to be thankful for what I have. A strong, healthy body, a good man. This dream I had of feeding the diggers, it is nothing. I am used to bigger disappointments—I have no children. But that is God's Will. Shall I tell you another of my secrets, since I have told you so much?'

'Yes, do.'

Polly sat on a high carved stool, the wood scrubbed and worn to satin whiteness. They had just finished a long morning's baking, and the good smell of newly baked bread and biscuits filled the kitchen. Katie was busy tidying up.

'I am a vain woman,' Anna confessed.

Polly hooted with laughter.

'Oh, Anna, what do you know of vanity?' she cried. 'That has always been one of my chief sins, so I can tell you that you are not vain, my dear.'

'Which shows that you do not know me. When I was a girl, before I married, I was for ever dressing-up and preening myself before my mirror. We lived in Cape Town, and I had many beautiful gowns. Oh, how I loved them, Polly! But now—look at me. My sisters, who still live at the Cape, would hardly know this drab hen I have become.'

Polly's eyes opened wide. With a cry she slipped from the stool and ran to her friend, impulsively taking her into her arms and hugging her.

'Anna! Anna!' she said excitedly. 'You have shown me a small way in which I can repay your kindness to us.'

Tom and Mutwa fetched the big black tin trunk from the wagon box, and set it down in Anna Viljoen's bedroom. Then the two women, and Samantha, shut themselves into the room, and Polly unlocked and raised the lid.

'We are much the same size. The gown will fit you perfectly,' Polly said breathlessly, shaking the lavender silk crinoline out of its tissue paper.

Arguments were overridden, and half-an-hour later Anna Viljoen was dressed in all her new finery, complete with bonnet and fan and French perfume.

'If Dan could see me!' she whispered. 'I cannot believe what I see.'

'Stay here. I will call him. Come, Samantha.'

'Oh, Tante Anna, you look beautiful!' Samantha said.

Polly Howes turned at the door. 'How old are you, Anna?' she asked. 'You look like a girl.'

'I am thirty-five. Believe me, Polly, girlhood is far behind me.'

'Just one year older than I!' Polly exclaimed. 'And now you look no more—if that.'

'We women age quickly. It is the hard life we live on the farms. But—Polly—I cannot believe—'

'It looks as though it were made for you. Now I will call Dan.'

Later, Dan Viljoen brought his wife in to show off her new elegance to Andrew Howes. He glowed with pride.

'Now you see the girl I married,' he said. 'What fine feathers will do. Of course we cannot accept such a gift without giving one also. It is our wish that you accept this farm, just as it stands.'

'You are certainly joking!' Andrew Howes laughed. 'The gown is a gift between women—between friends. I know the pleasure it has given Polly—'

'You will accept the farm,' Dan Viljoen said sternly. 'We know that the gown is a gift. Then so is the farm. It will free us to return to my brother's farm as soon as you are well enough to be left, Andries. We would never have found a buyer for this farm. We all know that very well. Now we have found someone who will—ag, man!' He changed his tune suddenly. 'What are words? Let us have no more of them in this business. The women have settled their affairs. We settle ours. Shake hands, man, the farm is yours—and I tell you I am glad to be rid of it.'

The quiet, slow-moving days were suddenly over. All was excitement, planning and hard work, and everyone was caught up in the happy chaos.

It was decided that Katie would remain at the farm, and no one was happier about the arrangement than were Katie and Mutwa.

'It is well for her to remain with you,' Anna Viljoen explained to Polly Howes. 'She is a Zulu, like Mutwa. On our farm at Potchefstroom she would be the only one of her race, and she would not like it there.'

'I have often wondered how she came to work for you?'

'We found her squatting here when we came. She had been brought up from the coast by an Englishman, and when he and his family all died of fever, Katie was stranded. So she built herself a hut and managed to live somehow until we came along and took her on to work for us.'

'What a blessing she will be to us!' Polly Howes exclaimed.

'Yes, she will. She knows how to cook English food, and I have taught her to prepare all the Boer dishes as well. She can make preserves, soap, candles, peach rolls, hippo bacon. There are few things she does not know in the kitchen. If you are really going to sell food to the diggers, as you say, she will be a great help to you, Polly.'

Mutwa was shown how to tend the poultry, how to kill and dress them for selling, and Dan Viljoen spent all the time he could spare instructing him.

'You will be able to run the farm from your easy chair on the stoep until you are about again,' he explained to Andrew Howes. 'I must take my boys with me, but you should be able to manage. If you need more boys later on you will have no trouble hiring them, although I advise you to keep an eye on them. I would never trust these local Kaffirs. I brought these boys with me when we came from the old farm.'

'I will be well again soon, and able to pull my weight,' Andrew Howes said.

'That's right, man, you will,' his friend agreed heartily.

'You will need a light wagon and mules to carry your things to Mac Mac to sell,' Anna Viljoen said one day, as Polly Howes and Samantha helped her with the seemingly endless task of packing. 'I have an idea which I shall discuss with my man. But first tell me, would Tom consider parting with that horse of his? I know he loves it. But I think he also knows that this is no place for an unsalted horse. When the hot weather comes it would probably be stricken and die overnight.'

'Yes, Tom does know that, Tante Anna,' Samantha said. 'We were talking about it yesterday. I know he's afraid of what might happen to Star.'

'Then perhaps my plan will work out.'

And work out it did. Much as it hurt Tom to part with his beloved Star, he saw at once that it would be better for it to leave the fever country. He also knew how invaluable the light mule wagon would be, and he accepted Dan Viljoen's offer of exchange gratefully.

'I have ridden Star about the farm, as you know, Tom, and I've enjoyed it. She's a fine mare and will be useful to me. And she has a better chance to live if she comes with us.'

Andrew Howes was thankful that he could in some measure repay the many kindnesses they had received, when it soon became clear that the Viljoens would need two wagons for their trek.

'Our wagon is comfortable for travelling, so I suggest you use it for that,' he said. 'Yours has stood unused for some time. Why not use yours to transport your stocks of hides and horns and ivory, and other goods? You cannot possibly manage with only one wagon, Dan.'

And so, after the usual argument, it was arranged.

'I will send the wagon back to you when we reach the farm. You will need it to carry all your gold down to the coast when you and Tom become diggers.' There was no accusation or bitterness in Dan Viljoen's voice, and Andrew Howes was glad of it. Only amusement. 'Each man must learn by his own follies,' he ended, as he had done so often before.

And so the day of their departure dawned. The women felt the parting keenly, and wept in each other's arms. But Polly Howes knew that some of her friend's strength of character would remain with her and sustain her in the difficult times that lay ahead.

'Magtig!' Dan Viljoen joked to hide his emotion, as he wrung Andrew Howes's hand. 'Never did I think I would be leaving this farm to a digger! Good luck, my friend.'

The big black trunk had again been stored in the wagon box, and as the Howes family and Katie remained on the stoep, watching the two wagons and Star slowly disappear over the mountain, Polly Howes thought of something her friend had said just before she climbed up onto the wagon seat.

'And so my wish is to come true, Polly? The foolish, hungry men will be fed with good food from these lands and this kitchen. What does it matter who does the feeding? I will now have no regrets. No regrets at all, dear friends.'

12

Mac Mac

'Now—to action!' Polly Howes cried, the huckaback towel she had been waving in farewell still clutched in her hand.

'Meaning?' her husband questioned.

'Mac Mac—what else?'

'*Cheers!*' Samantha shouted, dancing a jig. 'Oh, Mama, do you really mean—?'

'But you know I can't travel yet, my dear.'

'Oh, Andrew, of course I know. It breaks my heart that you're held up like this at the very last stage of the journey. But it won't be for long now. Every day you grow stronger. In another week I feel sure you'll be able to travel.'

'I'm quite sure of it. But what is this plan you have in mind, Polly?'

'Katie and I have a larder full of good things, and today we're going to start baking in earnest—Samantha, I depend on you. Early tomorrow Tom and Mutwa will set out for Mac Mac, with a wagonload of things to sell to the diggers. And to bring us back a true report on the place.'

'Only Tom and Mutwa? Surely I can go with them?'

'Samantha, be sensible. Remember the picture Dan Viljoen painted of the diggings—even though it may have been "tuppence coloured", as I suspect.'

'Don't worry, Sam.' Tom threw a comforting arm round his cousin's shoulders. 'If the diggers are men like Kangaroo Joe and Rollingstone Charlie—and why shouldn't they be?—it will be perfectly safe for you to come with us on the next trip. There may even be women there—probably are. Anyway, we'll be back the following day with a full report. Just think of it, Sam, I'll see Kangaroo Joe again!'

'Tom, I want a dozen fowls for roasting, and a quantity of fresh vegetables. Will you tell Mutwa, please, and see to that part of it?' his aunt cut in. 'And look out a few dozen eggs. Samantha, you must help Katie and me in the kitchen. There is so much to do, but I've got it all planned down to the last detail. Go along, all of you, I want a few words with my husband—alone if you please.'

Here again was the Aunt Polly who had kept them all on their toes in London, Tom thought, as he rushed off to find Mutwa. Her attitude towards Katie and Mutwa showed how completely free she was at last of the fears that had made her life in Pretoria so hard for her—and for her family—to bear.

As soon as they were alone Polly Howes went down on her knees beside her husband's chair and he gathered her into his arms. His face was alight with love for her.

'My wonderful Polly,' he said softly. 'You have lost your fear.'

'All of it, Andrew. At last I feel I can really live again. That I can enjoy this country. I believe—I believe I am as excited about the "yellow dirt" as you have been, my love, even though I know deep down that my heart will always belong to the city.'

From where she and Katie were busily preparing things in the kitchen, Samantha heard her mother's happy laughter, and suddenly everything was right with the world.

'Toss me an apron, will you, Katie,' she cried. 'We're going to make the best bread and pies those diggers have ever tasted.'

'Now I know why the Missus make Mutwa chop fire-wood as big as the house.' Katie shook with laughter as she rolled up her sleeves.

'What a good thing Dan didn't dream what was going on in your pretty head,' Andrew Howes chuckled. 'The dust hasn't yet settled from his wagon wheels—and here you are planning an assault on the diggings. It would have jolted him badly, I'm afraid.'

'But not his wife,' Polly smiled, scrambling to her feet and dusting her skirt. 'Anna would have loved every part of it. It was really her idea in the first place you know.'

Whenever they passed a digger slogging along beside his laden mule, or riding his horse, Tom shouted a greeting as though to a friend. Those who humped their swag mostly took short cuts across the veld, using the footpaths or beating their own tracks, and following the smell of gold almost as a crow flies.

September had got into its stride, and the veld was patterned with wild flowers, and lush with new grass. Giant tree-ferns grew in every crease in the hill-sides, and along every stream. Birds were spinning and darting or gliding on still wings against the high blue sky, and the air was pure and heady at that altitude, strong with the scent of mimosa and jasmine.

Mutwa sang in great voice to the rhythm of the mules' smart pace, and Tom thought he had never before known such complete happiness. He did not doubt that he would find gold, and the prospect of linking up again with Kangaroo Joe made him impatient to reach Mac Mac and begin his search for his friend.

The road swept round a shoulder of the hill—and there was Mac Mac before them. Weather-stained tents and all manner of shacks were dotted along the banks of the river that wound across the beautiful valley before it plunged three-hundred feet over the edge of the escarpment, to the Lowveld below. The roar of this waterfall sang in Tom's ears, and the activity all along the river, where diggers shovelled and panned, filled him with excitement. There were hundreds of men there, seemingly as busy as ants.

To the left of the road, built on the side of the hill, and commanding a perfect view of the two miles of meandering river, was a shack with a bold sign painted on the board that had been hammered on askew above the entrance—'The Spotted Dog'.

There were two men on the wooden veranda of the pub, and Tom was aware that they were watching his approach with interest.

One of them was unusually tall and slender, and even at that distance he gave the impression of elegance as he lounged against the veranda post, smoking a cheroot.

As they drew nearer, Tom saw that this handsome man wore sideburns, but was otherwise clean-shaven, and his clothes, although worn casually, bore the stamp of a good city tailor.

The other man sat on a beer cask smoking a pipe. He was older than his companion by a few years, Tom judged, and he looked like a prosperous digger who still followed the call of the Yellow Dirt, but no longer sweated on its trail.

'Pull over there, Mutwa,' Tom said. 'I think those gentlemen can help me.'

'Good day to you, young man,' the man on the beer cask called as Tom jumped down from the driver's seat and climbed the steep path. 'Now that's something I never expected to see. Dan Viljoen's wagon at the diggings! Well, well, what has got into the man?'

'Good day, sir,' Tom smiled, tucking his hat under his arm. 'The wagon no longer belongs to Mr. Viljoen. It is my uncle's—Andrew Howes—who now also owns the farm, Morenson.'

'So you see my information was right,' the tall man said to his companion. 'There's nothing wrong with my private spy-system I assure you. The enemy has flown. And in his place is a friend. A fair exchange.' He turned to Tom. 'And your uncle—?'

'He was wounded by a leopard. But he will soon be strong enough to come to the diggings himself.'

'I look forward to meeting him. But let us introduce ourselves,' the man on the cask smiled. 'My name is McLachlan, and my friend here is Mr. Herbert Rhodes.'

Tom's eyes shone.

'Of course we have heard of you. Who in South Africa hasn't?'

'And what, pray, have you heard of us? Come on now, the truth,' Herbert Rhodes challenged with a laugh.

'Well, sir, we heard that you own "The Spotted Dog"—'

'Yes, you would certainly have heard that from friend Viljoen. And that I am the ne'er-do-well brother of Cecil Rhodes, no doubt?'

Tom grinned. 'I know that Mac Mac is on your farm, Geelhoutboom, Mr. McLachlan. That you are the pioneer who first found gold in these parts.'

'That's damning enough—in the eyes of Dan Viljoen. Ah, here comes MacDonald—the Major is our Gold Commissioner. The first in this country, come to that. By the way, what's your name?'

'Tom Maxwell.'

'Maxwell, eh? And you have not told us your business here, Tom. If you're thinking of staking a claim—Why, good morning, Major MacDonald. This is Tom Maxwell, whose uncle has taken over Viljoen's place, and has become my neighbour.'

Tom had never seen such a colourful character as the Major. In fact, he could hardly believe his eyes. Well over six feet tall and straight as a rod, the man wore a wide-brimmed hat at a dashing angle over his long grey ringlets. Everything about him seemed larger than life, including the cigar clamped between his teeth. His wide belt was elaborately studded and buckled with silver, and he carried a silver-headed crop under his arm.

'Glad to meet you, Maxwell.' The Major clapped Tom on the shoulder and shook his hand as though it were the village pump. 'Any way I can help you?' His accent was American, his eyes friendly.

'Please, sir. I'm looking for a friend—Kangaroo Joe.'

'That's easy. See where the river takes a sharp bend over there?' Tom followed the direction in which the Major pointed, and nodded. 'You'll find your friend there. That's his claim. And that's his tent with the yellow patch on the side, pitched to the left of the crooked tree.'

'Thank you. Yes, I can recognize Kangaroo Joe on the river bank. That's his red shirt all right.'

'You aiming to stay here?'

'Not yet. I've brought a load of bread and pies and roast fowls, and eggs and vegetables, and some preserves. My aunt thought the diggers might—'

'Wow, now!' Major MacDonald exclaimed. 'Sounds like manna from heaven, eh McLachlan? Ah, I forgot, you've got a wife and home. Such things won't mean much to you. But to the rest of us—!' He scratched his chin. 'Of course there's the matter of a trading licence to be settled. That'll cost you all of £9 a quarter. And then there's another matter we must duly consider.'

'That the men haven't much ready money?' Herbert Rhodes broke in. 'They often pay in gold, Tom, and you would find that a difficulty.'

'Tell you what.' Major MacDonald had obviously found a swift solution to the problem. 'We'll buy what we need for our own use from you now. Then I advise you to offload everything else at McLeod's Store. He'll be glad enough to sell it for you on commission, or to buy it outright and sell it at a profit. The men would most likely mob your wagon if they knew what you had to offer. They're hungry men.'

'Thank you. That would simplify things. And the trading licence? I'm afraid I haven't £9 to pay for it.'

'Forget about it, my lad. Selling a few loaves and chickens to us isn't big business. And McLeod has a licence to cover the rest of it. You take what you want, Rhodes, and I'll ask you to drop my purchases over at my office, Tom. That's it, alongside my shack, over on the right bank of the river about a mile from here. Better still, I'll come up to McLeod's with you. I need to see him. Then we can go over to my place before you join Kangaroo Joe. A good man, that, by the way.'

'Tell your uncle that I'll be over to see him in a day or two,'

Mr. McLachlan said before Tom left with the Major. 'Unfortunately my wife and the girls are away visiting her people at the moment. But I'll be over anyway.'

Tom knew how his uncle would welcome the visit.

Although at first sight it seemed that the store was provisioned to the point of bursting outward under the pressure of stacked shelves, sacks of grain, and all the bulky impedimenta essential to a digger's way of life, Mr. McLeod was only too pleased to take all Tom had to offer. He gave a fair price under Major MacDonald's cool gaze, paying Tom outright, and ordering further supplies.

The wagon was empty except for the box of good things, carefully packed by his aunt and Samantha for Kangaroo Joe, when Tom left the Gold Commissioner's office with Mutwa, and headed the mules back towards Kangaroo Joe's claim.

Now that he was growing more accustomed to his surroundings Tom saw many things to which he had at first been blind. Among them the tents and lean-tos, and the men busily panning, even in the smallest creek of the many snaking down the hill-sides. He could now well believe Major MacDonald's estimate that there were one-thousand-and-thirty-five registered diggers in the area at that moment, with more arriving every day from D'Urban, Kimberley, and some even staggering in more dead than alive from the Death Trail from Delagoa Bay.

Kangaroo Joe was so intent on rocking his black iron pan, squatting at the riverside, that Tom stood beside him before he was aware of his shadow falling across the precious 'dirt' he was washing.

'*Strike me lucky!*' he roared when he squinted up into the sun-glare and recognized his visitor. 'If it ain't my mate Tom!'

Even in his excitement he laid his pan down carefully before seizing Tom's hand in both of his.

'So you've turned up at last, Tom? I said you would. An' jest in time, too. I pegged a claim for your uncle 'longside mine here. But I couldn't work 'em both. One had to go. But we'll stake another now you're here, an' I'll show you the ropes.'

'My uncle had an accident. That's what held us up. Have you had any luck at all, Kangaroo Joe?'

'Sure. Luck a'plenty. We don't shout about it, see? But this

here's a river of gold fair enough, like I said, Tom. Even new chums, who've never panned in their life, are stacking the yeller stuff away. That your wagon?'

Tom nodded.

'We brought a load of foodstuff from the farm to sell. Thanks to Major MacDonald I've got rid of the lot—all except the box I've brought for you, that is.'

'Farm, you say? Waste of time. Does that mean you don't aim to stay on here now?'

'I've got to get back to the farm in the morning, Kangaroo.

But my uncle reckons he'll be strong enough to make the journey to Mac Mac in a week's time.'

'Then you'll doss here tonight? Good. We can talk when I knock off. There's space for your wagon 'longside my tent. You get busy, lad. Those mules can get a feed, and I guess we can both swallow a mug of coffee. Haven't ate all day, come to think of it. Things is panning mighty lucky, and it's bad luck to break it up on a run like this.'

The smell of coffee and the sight of the meat pie Tom brought him prompted Kangaroo Joe to down his pan and tuck in.

'Ain't tasted grub like this, not since Pretoria,' he said, munching with satisfaction.

'Sam said to tell you she made them.'

'Bully for her. Your aunt come along too? Well, now, that sure surprises me.' Suddenly he raised his head like a war horse hearing a bugle call. 'Hey there—what's the commotion? Some'un's made a big strike! This is it, Tom. *This is it!*'

Everyone seemed to be running towards the knot of men gathered outside the Gold Commissioner's office.

'*Come!*' bellowed Kangaroo Joe, dropping his mug and legging it with surprising speed along the river bank.

'*Strike!*' '*Strike!*' '*Strike!*' echoed up and down the valley.

They were hoisting a man up onto an upturned soap-box when Kangaroo Joe and Tom arrived on the scene.

'That's—Bill—Trafford,' the digger panted. 'Lit out of Mac Mac—coupla days back. What the hell—?'

Major MacDonald came out of his office and forced his way to Trafford's side. He held up his hands to command silence and at once the uproar began to subside.

'Men!' he shouted. 'Quiet! William Trafford has news for you. Big news.'

The man on the box looked as though he were about to explode with excitement. Suddenly he dragged his hat from his head and kneaded it between his hands, and he seemed in danger of falling from his precarious perch. His eyes shot sparks.

'Speak up, Trafford!'

'Where's the Strike?'

'Shut up, can't you?' Major MacDonald ordered. 'The man's trying to tell you. *Shut up!*'

And this time they remained quiet while Trafford struggled to find his voice. It was a great moment in his life. Second only to the actual finding of his Eldorado.

'I climbed the high ridge yonder,' Trafford began, his voice pitched unnaturally high. 'From there I looked down on a valley —a deep, narrow valley, with a river—. What caught my eye first was the peach-trees all along the river banks. Fairest valley I ever saw—'

'*Gold!*' someone shouted in a voice like steam escaping from a boiler.

But now that he had started no one was going to spoil William Trafford's great occasion. There would never be another like it, that he knew.

'Something told me I'd arrived at last. Journey's end. Then I saw someone had got there ahead of me. Wheelbarrow Alec. But the blamed fool wouldn't talk. Wanted to keep it all to himself. Well, I moved along to a likely place—and started in panning the gravel.'

Everyone was so silent that the river seemed to roar.

Trafford's voice had sunk to little more than a hoarse whisper. 'There was gold in that first pan of dirt,' he said, and swallowed. 'Gold!' he suddenly yelled. 'Not just a tail of the yellow stuff— it was *thick with gold*. I went mad and kicked out at a rock in the river-bed in my excitement. It rolled over. *And there was this huge great nugget!*' He reached out and Major MacDonald placed the beautiful filigreed nugget in his shaking hand as though they had stage-managed the whole show. Trafford held it up for all to see.

'I started to shout to the mountains—the river—I wanted to shout my head off—"The Pilgrim is at Rest". And the echo came back clear and loud from the mountains, "*Pilgrim's at Rest . . . Rest*".'

William Trafford gulped, and his flow of words died in his throat as suddenly as it had gushed.

'And so,' Major MacDonald shouted so that all could hear, 'Mr. Trafford has called the valley Pilgrim's Rest. For all time, Pilgrim's Rest.'

Pandemonium broke loose.

'There'll be a stampede,' Kangaroo Joe shouted in Tom's ear.

'An' you won't see my trail for dust. You get back to the farm, Tom. Tell your uncle I'll be—'

'Better idea,' Tom shouted back. 'Let's drive over in the wagon. Quicker.'

'Fine, lad, fine! Two o' the best claims is what we want. I'll stake 'em and you can get on back here and register 'em with the Major first light tomorrow.'

The rush was on.

Two hundred diggers packed up their belongings on the turn

and trekked over the towering mountains. The rich strikes at Mac Mac were a thing of the past. Of hours past. Forgotten. They abandoned their claims without a second thought. Greater riches beckoned.

Soon they were spread out all along the stream that flowed through the deep valley.

Kangaroo Joe made for the middle reaches of the river, and there staked two adjoining claims, while Tom and Mutwa set up his tent and established camp.

Only one man among them was disconsolate. Alec Patterson watched the wild invasion of his peaceful valley with rage and sorrow. This slow-moving, taciturn character had pushed and pulled his worldly goods in a battered wheelbarrow all the way from D'Urban in his search for gold—and solitude.

In this valley he had at last found both his goals, in a setting more lovely than any he had ever seen in all his wanderings, with sweet water to drink, abundant game for the pot, even yellow cling-stone peaches to furnish a banquet in season.

Smoke from his fire was the first to rise before dawn the next day. He fried rhebok chops, brewed tea, and smoked his last pipe of tobacco.

Then he packed his wheelbarrow and stood sorrowfully on the river bank, listening to its voice which would haunt him to the end of his days.

'I'll be on my way,' he said to the valley. And spat into the rushing, crystal water, its sandy bed shining with grains of gold. Then he turned his back on it all, and trudged away behind his heavy, creaking barrow, his teeth clamped on the stem of his empty pipe so that their imprint bit into it.

13

River of Gold

The next morning Tom found it hard to tear himself away from the wild excitement that prevailed at Pilgrim's Rest.

A steady stream of diggers was marching in over the hills from Mac Mac and Lydenburg with fire in their eyes. They could hardly wait to dump their loads before rushing down to Pilgrim's Creek or the Blyde River to stake their claims.

The blows of hammers or pick-axe handles on the pegs that marked each claim, echoed up and down the sounding board of the valley, together with the shouts of men and frenzied labour with pick and shovel.

Already the banks of the streams looked like a giant pin-cushion, with pegs everywhere. These were long rods, projecting four feet above the ground claimed, and bearing a plate or piece of card on which the owner's name was written.

It was every digger's aim to span the stream with his 150′ x 150′ claim, so that part of the bank on either side of the water was included. And both the claims staked by Kangaroo Joe had this advantage. He had made very sure of that.

Nowhere in the narrow, winding valley was there as much as twenty square yards of level ground. Along the bed of the deep V meandered Pilgrim's Creek, the crystal water already churned to mud in many places. Where it met the wider Blyde River the Lower Camp was already taking shape. And on either side of the valley the mountains rose steeply, almost sheer above the stream.

'You be off, Tom, and get them claims tied up safe with the Gold Commissioner at Mac Mac,' Kangaroo Joe said, bolting the food Mutwa had prepared for them before the first rays of sun slanted into the valley. 'And you be back sharp, my lad.' His voice sank to a hoarse whisper. 'This here's something I never thought to see, Tom. Richest diggings in the world I'd say right now. Take a look at where the water laps the river bank—see the gold dust all along the water-mark? This here's the river of gold, Tom. Mac Mac had nothing on it. I tell you we'll make a fortune. We'll just rake it in. But be off—and get back here quick. *Get back!*'

'In the fastest time we can make it,' Tom promised.

He didn't know that the gold fire was already beginning to burn in his eyes, too. It was Mutwa who enlightened him.

'Ho, N'kosana, you get this white man's sickness too,' he said, laughing, as the mules valiantly hauled the wagon up out of the valley.

'Sickness? What do you mean, Mutwa?' Tom was startled.

'Your eyes—they shine like Baas Kang-loo Joe's eyes. Why are white men sick for this thing they find in the water?'

'It's gold, Mutwa. It means much money.'

'What good much money for you, N'kosana?'

'What good? Oh, Mutwa, you don't understand!'

Of all the darned silly questions, Tom thought impatiently, dismissing it. His mind was a turmoil of exciting pictures of the gold-flecked sands of the river, the huge nugget Bill Trafford had found—merely by kicking over a rock! The feverish activity along the valley, and the fortune he was quite sure they would find.

Because Tom remained silent, busy with his thoughts and plans, Mutwa began to sing, his powerful baritone voice ringing out across the veld and lending heart to the toiling mules.

There was some delay at the Gold Commissioner's office at Mac Mac, where men were hard-pressed about his shack, clamouring for their turn to stake their claims, pay their dues of five shillings a month, and be off. Waiting only long enough after attending to their business to mark the deal by bolting a couple of drinks at 'The Spotted Dog'—obligingly open at all hours on such occasions—before trudging back over the hills to where fortune awaited them.

Tom and Mutwa were nearing the farm when a bent and shuffling figure came in sight with a lame dog limping pitifully at his heels. They were obviously at the end of their strength, and although they were heading in the opposite direction, Tom, who was driving, pulled up as they approached.

'Anything we can do?' he shouted. 'You look caved in.'

As he stopped, the man's swag rolled from his sagging shoulders and thudded to the ground. He sank onto a boulder beside the trail. And the dog stood in its tracks, trembling, with tongue lolling out. Its ribs looked as though they might pierce its skin, and its paws were torn and bleeding.

Alarmed, Tom handed the reins to Mutwa, and leapt down. One close look at the man was enough.

'You're ill,' he said. 'Very ill. Here, Mutwa, lend me a hand, will you? We must get him into the wagon and make for home as quickly as possible.'

The man began to protest feebly and incoherently, but he passed out while being lifted into the wagon. To Tom's shocked surprise he felt like a parcel of bones, and Tom could have lifted him single-handed. The dog whined and staggered after them, and Tom picked it up and placed it beside the man before climbing up with them.

'Nothing we can do until we get them home. Mutwa, what is it?'

'Fever, N'kosana.'

Mutwa shook his head as he whipped the mules to their hardest pace, and Tom suddenly remembered some of the stories he had heard about the so-called Death Trail from Delagoa Bay, which led through fever country and crocodile-infested rivers, to the towering, seemingly impregnable wall of the Drakensberg, which must be scaled to reach the healthy air of the Highveld.

Could these two, the man and the dog, have made such a journey? Tom was appalled at the evidence of their suffering—and their endurance.

Not for one moment did he dream that he, too, would be making the terrible journey before many months had passed.

As he had lain awake through most of the previous night, rolled in his blankets in the wagon, and too excited to sleep, Tom had pictured his return to the farm. He had thought how he would break the news of Pilgrim's Rest and the claim that had been staked for them on the river of gold.

But now all that had to wait while the fever-stricken man was carried into the house, and his immediate needs were taken care of by Aunt Polly and Katie. Tom and Samantha gave their full attention to feeding and doctoring the emaciated dog.

There was only an opportunity for Tom to drop a few words to his uncle.

'There's been a great strike in a valley near Mac Mac, Uncle Andrew,' he said, pausing beside his uncle's chair. 'And we're in on it!'

'You mean—?'

'Kangaroo Joe's staked two claims—one for himself, and the one next to it for you. I registered them on my way back today. It's—it's—well, it's the biggest thing that's happened in this gold rush. They call the place Pilgrim's Rest, and they're rushing the valley from all quarters—it's unbelievable!'

'Tom—quick—I think the dog's dying!' Samantha cried from the enclosed veranda where Tom had carried the dog.

'Talk to you later, Tom,' his uncle called after him, clutching the arms of his chair in his excitement.

It was an hour before Tom was able to leave the dog and return to the front stoep, and then he saw that his uncle was in deep conversation with a visitor.

'Mr. McLachlan!' Tom exclaimed. 'Am I glad you've come!'

'I heard you'd registered claims and returned to the farm, so

I thought I had better come right over and see what was going on.'

'Did Uncle Andrew tell you there's a sick man—?'

'I've seen him, Tom. He'll pull through. We've had them stagger up from the Lowveld in even worse shape than that—and we've got them onto their feet again. How's the dog doing?'

'It was starved and exhausted. We've fed it, and Sam and I dressed its paws. How it managed to walk at all in that condition—!'

'From what I can make out from our friend in there—' Mr. McLachlan nodded towards the bedroom where the digger lay—'he came across the dog guarding the dead body of its master, somewhere along the Delagoa Bay trail. When he'd buried the man the dog followed him. Then he went down with fever. Usually these wrecks stop at my farm when they've dragged themselves up over the Drakensberg, but this chap missed it somehow. I've dosed him with "Dr. Livingstone's" physic, and he's sleeping now. I usually carry a bottle of the stuff with me. We all do. If one dose doesn't do the trick, you can start digging the grave.'

'Can Aunt Polly manage?'

'For the time being, yes. Your uncle has kindly invited me to stay the night, Tom. In the morning I will have the invalid taken over to my place. He'll be fit to be moved if he has a good night's sleep, and we're so used to taking care of men in his state that it's household routine, more or less.'

'Is Mrs. McLachlan back then?'

'Not yet, Tom. But we have a house girl who is a very good nurse. He'll be well cared for. And, of course, you folks will want to be on your way to Pilgrim's Rest as soon as possible. That's right I take it?'

Tom met his uncle's eyes and nodded. He felt excitement rising to choke him.

'And you've told Uncle Andrew about Pilgrim's Rest, Mr. McLachlan?'

'Of course. What else is anyone talking about, I'd like to know? Seems right now there's history being made in that valley.'

'I can't wait to get there!' Andrew Howes declared, forgetting his weakness and injuries for the moment.

His wife joined them, rolling down the sleeves of her blouse and smoothing her skirt.

'Isn't it getting chilly out on the stoep?' she asked, standing in the doorway. 'Do come indoors and have some hot coffee. It's all ready. Whatever it was you dosed the poor man with, Mr. McLachlan, it has made him sleep very soundly. Already I think his breathing is improved and his fever seems to be going down. Tom, will you give your uncle a hand? See, this chair is ready for him.'

Samantha had performed a lightning change of dress, and had brushed her hair. She danced into the living-room party-fresh in her pretty pink and white checked gingham dress with its wide pink sash, and a matching ribbon tying back her dark hair.

'Happy birthday to you,' she sang, grabbing Tom's hands and whirling him round. 'Happy birthday to you!—Happy birthday, dear Tommy.—Happy birthday to you!'

'Hey, what is all this? Sam—you're crazy!' he protested.

'Crazy, scatterbrain? If I don't remind you that it's your birthday today, you'll forget to remember that it's mine tomorrow,' Samantha laughed, kissing him before he could dodge away.

'Happy birthday, Tom!' His uncle held out his hand and Tom gripped it. 'This is one birthday you're not likely to forget.'

'Tom, dear, we had such a lovely surprise welcome all ready for you,' Aunt Polly laughed ruefully. 'I'm afraid all our plans were blown to the winds.'

'But the cake wasn't,' Samantha cried.

And Tom saw the splendid birthday cake set in the middle of the table, with '*Happy Birthday Sam and Tom*' inscribed in pink icing on top.

'It's a joint occasion for you two as usual,' his aunt said. And Tom remembered how he and his cousin had celebrated their birthdays together all down the years. How could he have forgotten Sam's birthday?

Gifts were heaped on a chair. A knitted jersey from his aunt, six beautifully hemmed handkerchiefs from Samantha, and a tin of sweets which Katie had made for him.

Samantha was opening her presents, with squeals of delight, holding up the pretty yellow crinoline her mother had secretly made for her, and the matching silk purse from her father, with a golden sovereign inside.

'Oh, Sam, forgive me!' Tom exclaimed. 'I have nothing to give you.'

'You gave me those lovely amethysts,' she reminded him gaily. 'And one day I expect you to have them cut and polished and made up into a necklace for me.'

'That I promise. Earrings too, and a bracelet.'

'I'll keep you to your word!'

'How old are you two?' Mr. McLachlan asked, enjoying the family scene.

'Fifteen,' Samantha told him.

'And high time you realized that you are a young lady,' her mother said with mock severity.

'Little chance of that I'm afraid, my dear,' Andrew Howes told his wife. 'If I know our daughter it will surprise me if she doesn't plan to become a digger wearing moleskin trousers, rather than a young lady entertaining beaux.'

'Heaven forbid! Andrew, what a dreadful thought.'

'Oh, but true, Mama. Quite true,' Samantha gaily assured her. 'I can't wait to get to Pilgrim's Rest and start working our claim.'

'And you won't be the first young lady to do just that,' Tom McLachlan told her.

'Oh, tell me, Mr. McLachlan! Do tell me about the others,' Samantha begged, absent-mindedly draping her lovely gown over the back of a chair without taking her eyes off their visitor.

'Samantha! All in good time,' her mother rebuked. 'Mr. McLachlan, do take a chair, and forgive our impetuous daughter.'

'Forgive? You forget that I have three daughters of my own, Mrs. Howes. All most impetuous.'

'And do they pan for gold?' Samantha demanded.

'Bless your heart, no. They've seen too much of it, my dear. But, believe me, they would if they thought it would be more fun than riding and dancing and picnicking, and entertaining an endless procession of suitors. You young people today do pretty much as you please, in my experience. Just as we did when we were young.'

'Samantha, come and cut the cake, dear. And a large slice for Katie and one for Mutwa, remember. Tom, will you hand the coffee round?'

The flow of talk went on and on, far into the night. Dinner replaced afternoon coffee. And they all sat round the living-room fire, plying their guest with questions and making plans. Now and again Polly Howes would slip away to check on the sick man's condition, but her reports were always the same. He slept like a log and his high fever was abating.

'You have told us how Mr. Trafford came to name the valley Pilgrim's Rest, but why did he call himself a pilgrim, Mr. McLachlan?' Polly Howes asked. 'Could it have had anything to do with *Pilgrim's Progress*?'

Mr. McLachlan's eyes twinkled.

'If you knew Bill Trafford you would hardly ask such a question, Mrs. Howes. He's a tough digger like most of the rest of them. I doubt if he has ever read a book in his life, let alone *Pilgrim's Progress*. When Herbert Rhodes and his party of twelve gay blades arrived at Mac Mac they called themselves the happy pilgrims. The name stuck and came into popular use. Now all the men digging at Mac Mac are known as pilgrims.'

'And this Herbert Rhodes,' Andrew Howes said. 'Dan Viljoen had some pretty hard things to say about him. Is there any truth in them?'

'Truth? Well now, it's hard to say. To a man like Dan Viljoen I imagine Rhodes must be a double-dyed villain. To most of us who know him, he's a most lovable man, popular with the diggers—with all of us, in fact. I'm not saying a word about his morals. They're none of my affair, you understand. But it speaks for itself that the men voted him onto the Diggers' Committee.'

'But this rumour that he is actually planning to sell a canon to Chief—Chief What's-his-name?'

'Secucuni—he's the Bapedi Chief, and we're expecting trouble from him. Yes, I have heard about that. And about his gun-running activities in general. It's very reprehensible, of course. Damned inexcusable, with things as they are here. But it's none of my business. We judge a man as we find him on the diggings, Mr. Howes. We don't sit in judgement on his past, nor on what he may be getting up to now—provided he toes the line in our community, and doesn't cause any kind of trouble. We deal pretty severely with trouble-makers, and of course thieves aren't tolerated. If a man is caught stealing from another digger he's given twenty-five lashes, half his beard and head are shaved, and he's run out of camp on the turn. If he dared to return, he'd be shot. Sorry, Mrs. Howes, we have to enforce a pretty ruthless code you know. What it means is that we have a most law-abiding, orderly camp. You'd find none better anywhere in the world.

'And we can thank the Australians for much of it. They came here with years of hard experience on their diggings behind them, and they knew how a camp should be run. They organized the Diggers' Committee, had a Gold Commissioner appointed, and made the laws that govern the camp.'

'These laws—?'

'They're very simple. Claims may only be worked from dawn to dark. No night work. That could lead to claim-jumping and stealing. No work on Sundays. There must be a day of rest. Dues must be paid on the nail—five shillings a month per claim. We've a good man in Major MacDonald. He's a most diplomatic chap, and to be trusted. When President Burgers visited us in August last year, he was most impressed with the order and general contentment among the diggers.'

'Kangaroo Joe says it was the President who named Mac Mac.'

'Quite right, Tom. It was typical of his humour. He's a grand man, President Burgers. Only trouble is, he's before his time. Progressive and an idealist.

'Well, he was running his eye over the register of claim-holders in MacDonald's office. "Just look at this," he said. "Two McDonalds, a MacDonald, two MacPhersons, MacTavish, MacAndrew. Why, it's all Macs. I'm going to call this place the Mac Mac Diggings from now on." Of course it's all part of the New Caledonia Gold Fields, you know, and Mac Mac is on my farm, Geelhoutboom.'

'Have you found gold on any other part of your farm?'

'Oh, yes. And I'd wager you'd find gold on your farm, too, Mr. Howes. There's alluvial gold in all these creeks and rivers. But some of it isn't in paying quantities, and at Mac Mac, and now at this new Pilgrim's Rest camp, there's such fantastic wealth of the stuff that there's no point in working the lesser fields.'

'Tom says that there are peach-trees at Pilgrim's Rest, Mr. McLachlan. However did they come to be growing there?'

'It's my guess that the dried peaches were brought up here by the Voortrekkers, and the pips were either planted or sowed themselves around their encampments. My family and I came to Geelhoutboom from Lydenburg via that valley, as a matter of fact, in 1872. It's a much easier route, but longer. And we saw not only many flourishing peach-trees along the Blyde River and the creeks down there, but also the remains of what had once been a homestead.

'Of course it was the Voortrekkers who called it the Blyde Rivier—the Joyful River—because it was there that a number of Boer women and children were reunited with their menfolk, whom they had believed had died or been killed on an expedition down into the Lowveld. They were trying to find a way through to Delagoa Bay—to the sea—but had been turned back by fever and the many terrible ordeals to be encountered on the Death Trail.'

'Mr. McLachlan, do tell us about the other women and girls at the diggings,' Samantha begged.

'Well, that won't take long. There are very few of them as yet, you know. And all of the white women are highly respectable, I assure you. My wife and our three girls were the first women here. Mr. and Mrs. Dietrich have recently arrived with their children. John and Mary Ann Purcell trekked from Kimberley, and then there are two sisters, Annie and Elizabeth Russell, who have just come from Pretoria to open a store for their father, whom you may know, Mr. Howes? I believe he has a trading store in the capital.'

'Why, yes, to be sure. And we know Elizabeth and Annie. I had no idea they intended coming to the diggings, did you, my dear?'

'No indeed. It will be delightful to meet them again. But have they come alone? Surely not.'

Mr. McLachlan laughed. 'I have only met Annie Russell once since they arrived a few days ago, but she strikes me as a most forceful young woman. Yes, they came alone. And I have a suspicion that their father's trading interests are likely to take second place. If I'm not mistaken, it's gold that has brought Annie Russell to Mac Mac, not the sale of merchandise.'

'Good for her!' Samantha cried. 'Imagine selling goods over a counter when one could be washing for gold.'

It was decided, over numerous cups of coffee, and more hours of discussion, that Tom and Mutwa would return to Pilgrim's Rest in the morning as soon as the wagon had been loaded with tents, food, picks and shovels, and other essentials with which they could set up camp.

'When Mutwa returns to the farm we will be ready to make the journey,' Andrew Howes said. 'If this chair is lashed into the wagon I should be quite all right. But we will have to travel more slowly, I imagine.'

'You do feel you can stand it, dear?' his wife asked anxiously.

'Let anyone try to stop me!'

'You could rest at Mac Mac if you found it too tiring,' Mr. McLachlan suggested. 'I know Rhodes would be only too happy to give you a shake-down—or Major MacDonald, for that matter. And this farm?'

'Mutwa and Katie can stay on here, and Mutwa can bring supplies of food over to Pilgrim's Rest several times a week—for our needs, and to sell. Katie knows how to run things here better than I do. We won't give up the farm, Mr. McLachlan. We have grown very fond of it.'

'That I can well understand, Mrs. Howes. You have a fine place here. I know how attached we have all become to Geelhoutboom, in spite of my wife's early misgivings about living so far from civilization.'

It was when Rocky Mountain Wilson, the fever-stricken digger, was being made comfortable in Mr. McLachlan's scotch cart the next morning, that Samantha had a stroke of luck.

'What about your dog?' Tom asked. 'You won't want to be parted with it, will you?'

The digger stared at Tom with unblinking, life-drained eyes.

'Dog?' he croaked. 'Dog? Ah, you mean that pesky mongrel what wouldn't be shook off no matter what? T'ain't no dog of mine. I buried his man. Can't feed mesself most times, how can I feed a dog?'

'Then we may keep him?' Samantha said, excited.

'Sure—keep him.' The digger closed his eyes as weakness overcame him, and that, as far as he was concerned, ended the matter.

'Oh, Tom, you said you hadn't brought me a birthday present,' Sam said. 'But you did. You did! I've been longing for a dog, and now I've got one. I'm going to call him Nugget—he's my first lucky strike. But not my last!'

14

A 'New Chum'

Tom found Kangaroo Joe working like a fanatic with crow-bar and pick when he arrived back at Pilgrim's Rest. His eyes were bloodshot and his sweat-soaked shirt was glued to his powerful body.

'It's these bloomin' great boulders, Tom,' he panted, almost reluctantly pausing to ease his laboured breathing and mop his streaming face. Sweat was blinding him. Impatiently, he pushed his hat onto the back of his head and mopped his face and neck with a strip torn off his old grey cotton blanket, which he used as a sweat-rag. 'Got to lever 'em out. Every jack one of 'em.'

'But why, Kangaroo? I thought the gold here was in the gravel.'

'Free gold, yes, for sure. We'll get that out by washin' the gravel from the bed 'n' banks of the stream. But it's nuggets I'm after, Tom. I've already heard tell of a coupla wopping great lumps o' gold that've come to light along this creek. Wedged down among the boulders they were, or dug out from under 'em.'

'You look all in. Have you had any food?'

'No time. I'll eat when we knock off. Come on, give me a hand here, Tom. Too much time wasted already. I'll teach you how to work a claim in smarter time'n any new chum ever caught on before.'

'Right. One moment though while I talk to Mutwa about what has to be done—'

'That can wait!'

Tom ignored what amounted to an order and ran back up the slope to where Mutwa was off-loading the wagon. Kangaroo Joe bellowed after him, but Tom chose to be deaf.

'Mutwa, I've got to leave all this to you I'm afraid,' he said. 'I'll help when I'm free. You do know what to do, don't you?'

Mutwa had missed nothing of the scene at the river. His eyes were very wise as he looked at Tom.

'Wah-me! This white man's gold-sickness!' he laughed ruefully. 'You go, N'kosana. But where you want me to put tents?'

'It all looks as steep as the side of a house to me. What do you think? I don't know anything about pitching a camp.'

Mutwa nodded.

'I make nice place,' he promised.

Knowing how much work would be entailed, Tom hesitated.

'But can you manage alone, Mutwa?' he asked anxiously, even as Kangaroo Joe's yell seemed to blast the ground from under his feet. 'Coming!' he shouted back.

'You go, N'kosana. Baas Kang-loo Joe's belly hungry. Make him angry. You go now.'

Quickly Tom stripped to the waist and kicked off his velskoen before running down to the river. He rolled his corduroys up above his knees as he joined Kangaroo Joe in the water. He was surprised that the miner splashed about in his hobnail boots, his moleskin trousers soaked to the knees. Tom noticed that most of the men on neighbouring claims worked with the same complete disregard for personal comfort, engrossed as they were in the one thing that mattered to them—their search for gold.

Kangaroo Joe grunted and gave Tom a distinctly sour look.

'We've got work to do, and don't forget it,' he said.

Tom met his eyes coolly. 'You tell me what to do and I'll get on with it,' he said. 'My people will be coming here tomorrow or the day after, and I've got to have things ready for them.'

Kangaroo Joe straightened up, and for the first time managed to grin.

'See here, Tom, I'm tetchy. Take no notice. It gets one this-away. But we've got a powerful big job t'tackle if we're going to work this claim right.' He broke off suddenly, his eyes trained beyond Tom. 'What in heck goes on?' he demanded.

Tom turned to see.

'It's only Mutwa lighting a fire to boil the billy,' he said. 'He reckons you need food.'

'Waste of time! But look here, Tom, I don't want no more coffee, y'understand. Hate the stuff. Tea's the poison on the diggings. Coffee's what the Boers drink. Don't begin to touch a man's thirst. Tea's the only substitute fer the real McCoy.'

'I don't think we have any tea.'

'Then get some from my tent—if we've got to stop fer food. Tom-fool nonsense! You'll find some in a baccy tin in my tent, 'longside the bed. Give it to yer boy, but tell him to go easy. It's all I got.'

When Mutwa brought them mugs of tea and thick chunks of bread and cold meat, Tom saw how ravenous his friend was. Kangaroo Joe bolted the food and held out his mug to be refilled. They sat on the river bank, and Kangaroo Joe stared at the water as though hypnotized.

When he got to his feet he stretched his arms above his head and let out a long sigh of relief before picking up his crow-bar and stepping down into the water.

There was little said during the next few hours. Tom had never worked at such a furious pace in his life, and he needed all his wind for the job.

Together they laboured to divert the water into a narrow channel they dug, called a 'water-race', so that they could work on the river-bed. The top soil, consisting of fine sand, had to be removed with shovels and thrown up onto the bank of their claim, to be worked over later.

It was only at sundown, when all work had to stop on the diggings, that Kangaroo Joe could answer Tom's questions as they ate the meal Mutwa had prepared for them.

'Give me some idea of how a claim's worked, Kangaroo Joe. I'm working blind right now and not much of it makes sense.' Tom rested his aching back against a boulder as he spooned the stew from his tin plate.

Under the top soil on the river-bed was the layer of wash and boulders which contained the gold, Kangaroo Joe explained. Often there were two layers of gold-bearing wash and boulders, which meant digging deep. Over the ages the gold had been carried down by the stream and had sunk through the soil and settled above the bed-rock. Nuggets and pockets of coarse gold tended to be held up by the boulders and were, therefore, often found beneath them. That was why a very careful search was made whenever a boulder was moved from its bed. And the river gravel was all removed and washed carefully.

Their first job in the morning would be to make a sluice-box.

This, Kangaroo Joe explained, was a long, coffin-shaped construction made of wood, 20 feet or more in length, 18 inches wide and 18 inches deep. He had already bought the wood and it was stored in his tent. At the bottom of this sluice-box slats of wood were nailed transversely across the 'floor' plank to form what was known as a 'Venetian ripple'.

The gravel, earth and small stones taken from the claim were shovelled into this box and the water from the 'race' was then led through it with a good 'head' on it. The 'spoil' was washed straight through the box and out at the far end. But the gold, being heavier than the gravel, sank to the bottom of the box and was caught by the slats that formed the 'ripple'. If the gold was particularly fine, a blanket or sheepskin was placed at the bottom

of the sluice-box so that the fine particles of gold could be caught in the hair.

The great moment of the digger's day came when he 'cleaned up'. Here the big man's eyes blazed with excitement. The mud and fine stuff at the bottom of the box were then carefully scraped out and panned in a skilful process of rocking and tilting the iron basin until finally all the mud and pebbles were tipped out and nothing was left but the *tail of gold*—the day's takings.

This final process produced the gold-dust, which might weigh a couple of pennyweights or as much as eight ounces.

Of course nuggets were spotted earlier in the proceedings, picked out, washed, and popped into the tin or bottle kept for the precious horde. Or, if the nugget was a wopper, it was hidden in the digger's shirt until he got it safely to his tent, when it was salted away in a secret place until it could be deposited with the Gold Commissioner.

And how much was a pennyweight of gold worth? Tom wanted to know.

'Three-an'-sixpence to three-an'-nine. Depends on the quality,' Kangaroo Joe told him. 'And an ounce of the yeller dirt's worth three-pound-ten.'

As soon as their meal was over, Tom pitched into the work of helping Mutwa to create order out of the chaos that was around them. Ground had been levelled with much spade-work during the afternoon, and Mutwa had actually erected the tents single-handed. It remained to dig a storm-water ditch around each tent and get the little furniture they had brought with them under cover.

It was dark long before they had finished the job, and they worked on by the faint light of hurricane lamps.

When at last Tom fell onto his camp bed, fully clothed, he slept immediately, and he didn't know that Kangaroo Joe came into his tent to pull off his velskoen and throw a thick blanket over him.

Tom felt as stiff as a board the next morning when Mutwa awoke him at cock-crow with his breakfast. The tea had tasted so strongly of tobacco the day before that he was relieved to find coffee in his mug.

'I take tea to Baas Kang-loo Joe,' Mutwa said, smiling.

The mules were already harnessed and Mutwa left for the farm as soon as the meal was over.

If all was well with his uncle, Tom could expect the family to arrive the next day, or the day after. He realized that it was going to be tough going to keep pace with Kangaroo Joe's demands now that the golden bit was between his teeth, and he would welcome their presence.

Before starting work, Kangaroo Joe sliced a glob of plug tobacco from the roll he kept on the milk box beside his bed, and stuffed it into his cheek.

'Helps a man, having somethin' to chew on when he's working,' he said. 'Keeps off the pangs of hunger.'

Tom grinned. 'I've heard it said that food does the same thing,' he said.

'Waste of time, knockin' off fer meals when there's a gold rush on. Chance of a lifetime, this here.'

They were hard at it half-an-hour later, constructing the sluice-box, when the digger working the next claim up-stream went berserk and brought all work in their immediate section to a stop.

His yells echoed up and down the valley, and there he was performing the strangest acrobatics in the shallow water that flowed through his claim.

He was a bandy-legged little chap with a bald head and flowing white beard, who had reminded Tom of a gnome at first sight the day before. Now he was hugging something to his chest while he leapt about and yelled his head off.

Kangaroo Joe looked as though he had turned to stone for one long second while he watched his neighbour's performance. Then he, too, appeared to go mad.

Tom stared in petrified amazement as his friend strode across to the man and delivered a powerful punch to his jaw that sent him sprawling. It knocked the digger cold, and Kangaroo Joe picked him up and carried him to the bank of the stream, dumping him on the grass without ceremony. The man's arms were still clasped round what looked to Tom like a large stone.

'What have you done?' Tom demanded. 'You could have killed him. What's wrong, Kangaroo?'

'He'd have bust a blood vessel, or gone clean crazy if I hadn't knocked him out. I've seen this happen before when—when— D'you see what he's found? A fortune!'

Others had come running and were crowding round the unconscious man, their eyes wide and shining, and an edge to their voices that Tom was coming to recognize.

'Cor—look at it!' the Bos'n said with awe. 'Great golden *boulder*, that's what he's found. Bet it weighs every ounce of thirty pounds!'

His guess was out by five pounds. That nugget tipped the scales at just over twenty-five pounds, and was the first of many lucky strikes that shook even hardened diggers by the size and quality of the nuggets.

Nuggets were being found from the first in all shapes and sizes, and they had two unique qualities. Many had been so weathered that they had formed strangely beautiful filigree patterns, and looked like the finest Indian craftsmanship. Small ones were often mounted as they were into brooches and pendants, and became extremely valuable. And the nuggets of Pilgrim's Rest gold had a curious pale radiance found nowhere else in the world. It was real 'ash-blonde' gold, the colour given it by the high percentage of silver it contained in its raw state.

It was not to be wondered at that men came flocking from all over the world as soon as the story spread abroad of the Eastern Transvaal Gold Rush.

After that first big find on the next claim there was no holding Kangaroo Joe. Had it not been strictly enforced that no digger could work longer than the ten hours from dawn to dusk, Tom believed he would have driven himself—and Tom!—round the clock.

In those early days no Africans were employed on the diggings in the Pilgrim's Rest area. This was due to the fact that many of the diggers were Australians who preferred to do their own work or employ their own kind, which made the alluvial gold-mines vastly different from the diamond mines at Kimberley, which largely depended upon 'black labour' from the first.

The sight of the familiar mule wagon approaching down the steep road leading into the valley gave Tom a greater lift than any nugget would have done at that moment. He was exhausted and hungry, although making every effort to hide the fact from Kangaroo Joe.

Fortunately it was nearing sundown so Tom felt he could down pick and shovel and call it a day with a clear conscience.

The journey had taxed the strength of Andrew Howes, and he was obviously thankful to be helped into bed as soon as his wife had prepared it.

Samantha was wild with excitement, and Tom was surprised to see how her dog Nugget had recovered in so short a time. He shadowed his mistress, always close at heel.

It was amazing the transformation that took place in the camp before nightfall. Instead of simply being a group of tents in a sprawling tent town on the lower slopes of Theta Hill, it became a home. In addition to the three bell-tents already erected, which were to be their bedrooms, a marquee tent was quickly put up to provide a living-room and kitchen.

Polly Howes was like a general marshalling her forces, while working at top pressure herself. She had planned exactly where every item of furniture was to be placed, and in Samantha, Tom and Mutwa, she had a splendid team.

'I can't wait to get started in the morning,' Samantha said when they were all enjoying the good food Katie had prepared at the farm, which was heated up. The warm yellow glow of the lamps filled the tent, making the night beyond the open tent flaps appear mysterious and inky black. 'If only we'd been able to get here in time to have a real look at the claims while there was light.'

'Cock-crow will come soon enough, take it from me,' Tom assured her. 'But are you sure Uncle Andrew will be all right, Aunt Polly? It's a rough drive over that track.'

His aunt had just returned with her husband's tray.

'He's almost asleep already, Tom. He needs rest. His wounds haven't knit well yet, and his back gives him a good deal of pain. But he wouldn't hear of our postponing the journey. If only there were a good doctor here.'

'Waal, there are doctors here at that,' Kangaroo Joe drawled. 'But they'd take a power of sobering up before they'd be able to tell a sick man from a well one. And they're not too keen to be pulled into the picture.'

'Do you mean to tell me that there are qualified doctors here in Pilgrim's Rest?' Polly Howes demanded with disbelief.

'Sure there are. Two that I know of, and it's likely others are playing possum and don't let on they're quacks.'

'But why, in heaven's name?'

'Simple enough. They *was* doctors. Now they're diggers. Makes all the difference. Only two things matter with the pair I know of. One's gold, and t'other's liquor. Nothin' else means anything to either of them any more. James Ashton, f'instance. He's a dingkum surgeon. But look here, ma'am, you ask Major MacDonald or McLachlan when they come over in the morning. There's going to be a meeting to elect a Diggers' Committee, same as we had at Mac Mac, so they'll be here all right.'

'You've given me new hope, Kangaroo Joe! If these men really are qualified doctors, and it is just a matter of sobering them up—'

'There's soberin' up and soberin' up, ma'am,' the Australian tried to forewarn Polly Howes. 'An' you can take it from me these chums are dead set against such an operation being performed on them. It costs more than a mite to get mortilation spifflicated, which is the way they are most times while the money hangs out. They wouldn't take kindly to havin' the good work undone jest so's they could be made to do work they don't want to do no more. Stands to reason. But you see McLachlan. He'll tell you how it is better'n I can.'

The fact that there were qualified doctors in the valley was the best news Polly Howes could have had, and she was in high spirits when they each took their lighted lantern and closed the flaps of the marquee for the night.

Sounds carried with astonishing clarity in the narrow valley, and men's voices could be heard arguing, declaiming, and in bursts of song to a mandolin accompaniment.

Underlying the human sounds there was the eternal lullaby of the river, and the night wind gently hushing through the grass.

'The lights in the tents look like hundreds of fireflies,' Samantha said as she stood outside her tent with her mother's arm about her shoulders. 'Oh, Mama, how can we possibly sleep tonight? I've never in my life felt so excited. Just look up, Mama! It's as though the stars form a ceiling over this deep valley, stretching from one hill-top to the other.'

Polly Howes laughed softly.

'There's certainly magic here, Sammy dear. I don't wonder the river sands are powdered with gold as Tom says. And this wonderful air! Now that I know your father will be in a doctor's care I feel sure everything will come right for us.'

'Sleep well, Sam,' Tom called before entering his tent. 'You'll find out what work is in the morning!'

'As though I don't know! 'Night, Tom. Good night, Kangaroo Joe. You'll have another "new chum" on your hands tomorrow.'

When Nugget settled down beside Samantha's camp bed he thumped his tail on the ground and made strangely conversational noises in his throat. He was certainly a happy dog.

'I know how you feel, Nugget,' Sam told him, reaching out to pat his head. 'This is your kind of life, isn't it, boy? I believe you can smell gold like a regular digger. Good night, mate.'

15

Tent Town

'If Mutwa can give us a hand for a coupla days, we can get the work on your claim started,' Kangaroo Joe said the next morning. 'If claims aren't worked they're taken over, so we can't hold fire any longer, ma'am. I'll show him what's to be done, and Tom's had a bit of experience already. It's a matter of digging the water race first go off, and starting to shovel the top soil away. Just hard slog. Some uncommon big boulders on your claim, too. They'll take a lot of budging. My sluice-box'll do for the two claims till we've time to knock another one together.'

'Of course Mutwa can stay on for a few days. Katie can manage things on the farm until he gets back. But please don't let our claim be too great a burden, Kangaroo Joe. You have your hands full working your own.'

'We're in this game together, ma'am. Two claims it is.'

'You're a dear!' Samantha said with feeling. 'We'd have been lost without you.'

In spite of her mother's misgivings, Sam wore trousers for the first time in her life. She had taken in a pair of Tom's corduroys so that they fitted her, and wore one of his shirts, the sleeves of which she had cut off above the elbow. And she wore her hair in two plaits tied with red ribbon. Her mother had insisted that she wear one of the shady Boer sunbonnets, called 'kappies', which Anna Viljoen had left for Polly to wear on the farm.

'How will I know when Mr. McLachlan arrives, Kangaroo Joe?' Polly Howes asked anxiously. 'I don't want to miss him.'

'You won't, ma'am. I'll tip you off. The meeting's at knock-off time this evening, but they'll be here some time during the day. Come on—it's *work*!'

And work it was, with a vengeance, as Samantha soon learned. At first she could hardly believe her eyes when Tom pointed out the gold-dust in the river sand, and how her toe-nails glittered with the bright particles after she had been working in the water for a short spell.

Before the morning was out it was the blisters on her hands that claimed her attention, and the fact that her back was 'broken'.

'You'll toughen up soon enough,' Kangaroo Joe told her. 'Every new chum has to be broken in. Say if you want to quit, Sam.'

'*Quit?* Never! What an idea.'

Andrew Howes had been made as comfortable as possible in his armchair. The flaps of his tent had been tied right back so that he was in the shade and yet had a clear view of the river below, where Kangaroo Joe, Tom and Mutwa were working tirelessly, and Samantha was doing her best to keep pace with instructions.

He felt bitterly frustrated and helpless, and the painful after-effects of the drive added to his depression.

'I should never have brought you here, Polly. It was sheer madness,' he said. 'Where on earth will it all end now?'

'I will tell you, Andrew.' His wife sat down on a stool beside him. 'It's going to end in our finding a fortune. And then—who can tell? When the novelty of this rough life wears off, the call of civilization may well draw us back to the old life we knew. We just don't know, Andrew. But I do know that as soon as you're better everything will look differently to you, my dear. When Mr. McLachlan arrives—'

'And what will happen then, pray?'

Neither of them had heard Mr. McLachlan's approach, and they looked up, startled, at sound of his amused voice.

'Oh, how welcome you are, Mr. McLachlan!' Polly Howes cried. 'Kangaroo Joe says there are qualified doctors here in Pilgrim's Rest. Is it true?'

'Well, yes, it's true enough, Mrs. Howes.' He sounded dubious.

'My husband needs the attention of a doctor. Will you kindly tell me where I can find one?'

'It's not as easy as that, you know. One of them's holed up in a cave near the top of Theta Hill with a cask of Jamaica rum. Until the cask's empty there is nothing at all we can do about Jamaica Bill. And I doubt if he would be much use sober these days. He's pretty far gone I'm afraid.'

'Is he really a qualified doctor?'

'Certainly. Highly qualified. And he came out here with the best intentions in the world, I believe. But the gold bug bit him and he struck it rich unfortunately. It proved too much for him. Sudden wealth often proves fatal to a weak man. Now he's in the process of drinking away his wealth. Then he'll no doubt sober up of necessity and start fossicking for another fortune in gold. It's happening all the time, Mrs. Howes.'

'And is he the only one?' There was a note of desperation in Polly Howes's voice.

'Oh, no. There's a young Lancashire doctor down the valley who is a much more likely bet. James Ashton. He's taken what the Scots call a "scunner" at doctoring, and he's a good chap at heart. I happen to know that he's a graduate of Trinity College, Dublin. When first he pitched up at Mac Mac he was willing enough to follow his proper calling. He saved many a life. But unfortunately several serious operations he undertook went wrong. The men died under his knife. Mind you, he was working under very bad conditions, lacking the proper appliances, and with rough and ready methods of nursing. It probably wasn't his fault. But he couldn't stand it. Took to the bottle, and became a digger. Refused point-blank to do any more doctoring.'

Hope had died in Polly Howes's face.

'Mind you, if we can sober him up, and prevail on him to co-operate, he could at least examine you, Mr. Howes. As a matter of fact I noticed when I passed by just now that he has actually put up a sign outside his tent. Looks hopeful. It reads, "JAMES ASHTON. SURGEON, BARBER, TENTMAKER".'

'He can't be serious! Are you quite sure he *is* a medical man and not a fraud?'

'Quite sure. I've seen his certificate.'

'Then it looks as though we'll just have to let Nature work the trick,' Andrew Howes said. 'Frankly, I don't fancy having either of the men you've mentioned doctoring me.'

'You may be right. But I'll see what I can do. Ashton could at least examine you and give an opinion—if we can dry him out. You'll probably feel much better when the effects of that drive have worn off. Why, bless my soul! Is that Samantha working down there on your claim?'

'I'm afraid it is.'

'No "afraid" about it. It will do her good. These young people need an outlet for their energies. And who isn't being affected by this Gold Rush?'

Polly Howes met his eyes and felt her colour rising.

'You're right,' she admitted. 'Samantha had her way because I understood how she felt. This gold-fever has no respect for one's age or sex I'm afraid.'

'Too true. I saw Annie Russell working her claim with all the energy and concentration of a man just now. And of course Mrs. Lilley always wears male attire. She and her husband work a claim in the Upper Camp.'

'Oh, Mr. McLachlan, what must you think of me?' Polly Howes exclaimed. 'What a way to welcome the first visitor to our tent home! Why I haven't even offered you a chair or refreshment.'

'Think nothing of it, Mrs. Howes. I had time to spare before our meeting this afternoon, and I wanted to see how things had fared with you good people.'

'Then you will have lunch with us. I was on the point of preparing it.'

'I'd be glad of your company if you can spare the time,' Andrew Howes said. 'There are many questions I'd like to ask you.'

Polly Howes left the two men smoking and talking while she busied herself in the improvised kitchen. She was bitterly disappointed, for she had attached great hope to the possibility of obtaining skilled medical care for her husband.

It was Major MacDonald who again revived hope when he looked in a little later, ostensibly to see how they were settling in, but readily accepting an invitation to share their meal.

'What shape's young Ashton in?' McLachlan asked.

The Major raised his eyebrows at the question.

'Much as usual. Pickled. Why do you ask?'

'Our friend here needs medical care. Think there's any chance of sobering Ashton up for the job?'

'Only one way to do that, and I'm not sure it's legal. We'd have to put him in stocks for a couple of days. But wait a moment! A doctor, eh? A new chum registered a claim with me this morning.

Admitted he was a medico—not over anxious to share the secret, mind you, but, well, it came out. I gave him a lift here from Mac Mac, as a matter of fact, and we got talking. He doesn't look like a soak, anything but, only—well, you never can tell, can you? Reckon I'll rope him in right now before he has time to wet his whistle.'

'He—he could have lunch,' Polly Howes suggested, hopefully offering her bait.

'Hold everything. I'll be right back with this character, hog-tied or running free.' And the Major was off at a quick stride down the footpath leading along the river's edge to the Lower Camp.

'Samantha!' Polly Howes called. 'I need you, dear.'

She could cope with the appetites of her family, but this meal was growing beyond all expectations. Not for the first time in the past weeks Polly Howes thanked providence for Katie and the food she had prepared in the big farm kitchen.

Dr. Somers came reluctantly, but he came. And, after enjoying the best meal he had eaten in months, he was willing enough to examine Andrew Howes and attend to his injuries. He proved to be a very charming young man, and was on easy terms with the family before the meal was over.

'I make only one proviso,' he said. 'It must not get around that I'm a doctor. I have sound reasons, I assure you, and I have no cause to be ashamed of them. But I'm here as a digger. Will you accept that?'

'But of course,' Major MacDonald assured him. 'I take it as a personal favour that you're willing to help Mr. Howes here.'

His instrument case and medical supplies Dr. Somers unpacked from the rucksack he had carried casually slung over his shoulder.

Although Kangaroo Joe, Tom and Mutwa had returned to the river immediately the meal was over, Samantha waited to hear the result of the examination, and to be on hand should her mother need her. While she waited nervously she washed up the pile of dishes and tidied up.

As soon as Polly Howes emerged from the tent Samantha flew into her arms.

'Oh, Mama, it will be all right!' she cried, reading her mother's face.

'Everything will be fine,' the young doctor said, smiling at her. 'Your father was in considerable pain because some of his wounds needed attention. Now that they're clean they should heal without further trouble.' He turned to Polly Howes and held out his hand. 'I'll call in again to make sure everything is going well. If you need me I'll be glad to come.'

'Thank you, Dr.—'

'Not that, please! My name's Richard Somers.'

'We won't forget—Richard. And please, any time you feel like home cooking, know that you will be more than welcome to join us here.'

'That's an invitation I'll certainly bear in mind. Thank you, Mrs. Howes.'

Major MacDonald rose to join him. 'I'll come along with you, Somers,' he said. 'I'd like to see that claim of yours. You coming, McLachlan?'

That day proved to be a lucky one all round. Kangaroo Joe found a nugget weighing three pounds, and two small filigree nuggets of great beauty, in addition to a most satisfactory haul of fine gold at the clean-up.

A branch of the Natal Bank had opened for business that morning, the wood and iron building having been run up almost overnight on the edge of Pilgrim's Creek. Diggers took their gold straight from their claims to be weighed on the scales in the back yard, from where they passed inside to receive cash or credit for it.

Kangaroo Joe had never before in his life had an account at a bank, preferring to carry his gold about with him, but Major MacDonald had persuaded him to bank it.

He would not part with the filigree nuggets, however, and stored them with his 'Burial gold' in a large Colman's mustard tin. There was a superstition among diggers concerning the ounce or two of gold that was kept in a pocket by day, under their head as they slept, for without it a dead man was given a pauper's burial, which was a crowning disgrace, and considered 'unlucky' into the bargain.

The meeting that sundown caused great excitement, and it drew most of the inhabitants of Pilgrim's Rest to the so-called Market Square, which was then no more than a rough patch of hill-side in the process of being levelled off. Wagons outspanned there, but no tents could be erected.

The speakers climbed onto a wagon which acted as a platform, and Major MacDonald was elected chairman. This was as well, for if anyone could control the high-spirited crowd he was that man.

Samantha had changed into a frock and was there with Tom and Kangaroo Joe, and she was thrilled to see a few women's kappies among the forest of battered felt hats worn by the men. She waved and smiled at the Russell sisters, but couldn't get near enough to speak to them.

All of the men elected onto the Diggers' Committee were strangers to Samantha, but she clapped and cheered with the rest as each man clambered up onto the wagon and had his say.

Tom struck up an acquaintance with a young man standing next to him. He looked no older than Tom, and was very slight and fair, with shy blue eyes and a nice smile.

When the business of the meeting was over and the milling crowd began to break up, most of them made for the several pubs to drink the good health of the new Diggers' Committee.

Every day a new pub seemed to open in the valley. Sometimes it was no more than a tent, but more often a shack was knocked together conveniently near the claims. YE DIGGERS' BAR, OUR HOUSE, TOM CRADDOCK'S BAR, THE HALFWAY HOUSE and STENT'S CATHEDRAL were among the first to go up, and they all did a roaring trade. Most of them even employed a 'runner' who was always ready to deliver a bottle to a claim when a digger wanted to celebrate a lucky strike or drown a disappointment.

'Who were you talking to, Tom?' Samantha asked as they hurried home along the track that had been beaten seventy-five yards above the creek, and running parallel to it. The few shacks that had already gone up faced onto this track, and there the storekeepers were pitching their tents. In the roughest possible sense, it was Main Street, Pilgrim's Rest, and destined to remain so for at least a hundred years.

'Will Scully. He's a very decent chap. I saw him when he walked into camp the other day. He's got courage, Sam!'

'What has he done?'

'He's on his own here, and he only had seven shillings in the world when he got here after walking all the way from Kimberley. He's taken a job working for a party of Australian diggers for his keep. He's been diamond mining at Kimberley, but had no luck. And he's quite new to gold-mining. Apparently the two kinds of mining are quite different. He wants to learn how to work a claim, and of course he must save a few pounds before he can stake one on his own.'

'It's a pity he's not being paid for his work then.'

'This is just the beginning. As soon as he's had a little experience he'll be able to sell his labour for hard cash.'

'But he doesn't look any older than you, Tom.'

'Oh, but he is. He said he was nineteen. It's just that he's such a thin little chap. I think we're going to be friends.'

And friends they soon became. They met the next day at James's Store, Tom to buy a new pick handle, while Will had to buy provisions for the Australian diggers who employed him, and pay their monthly acount.

No stores were paid with ready money. Bills were delivered by hand on the last Saturday of every month, and they were expected to be paid on the following Monday. Gold-dust was taken instead of coin, and it was the storekeeper's right to 'blow the dust' on the scales. One ounce of gold-dust was worth £3.10*s*.0*d*.

Tom watched Joe Barret, Mr. James's assistant, blow the gold-dust Will carefully tipped into the pan of the scales from the tin he carried in his pocket.

'What about the gold-dust that's blown onto the floor?' he asked.

Joe Barret grinned.

'I'll tell you, mate,' he said, obviously proud of himself. 'When we was laying a new mud floor at Mr. James's store at Mac Mac, before we moved on down here, I said how about us putting the old floor through the sluice-box. Well, we did, see. And you know how much we cleaned up? Forty quid's worth of pure gold. So you see there's method in this blowing of the scales.'

'You doing anything special on Sunday, Tom?' Will asked when they left the store and had to go their separate ways.

'Not that I know of. Why?'

'I always go for a walk on Sunday. Stretch my legs. If you'd care to come with me you're welcome.'

'If I'm not needed I'd like that. Thanks, Will. See you then.'

That was to be the first of many Sunday walks which the two had together, and their friendship deepened.

Tom would take a double lunch and the two young men would walk to the top of the 'Divide', which was the backbone of the towering mountain range. On one side of it lay Pilgrim's Rest, on the other Mac Mac, and on clear days they would have far, faint glimpses of the mysterious Lowveld, which was just visible over the intervening precipice-edge plateau which lay beyond the Mac Mac and Waterfall Creeks.

The Lowveld beckoned Will Scully and he was determined to explore it one day. Often he would dream aloud as they sat high above the tents of men, until Tom caught some of his restless, adventurous spirit and wanderlust, and felt the spell of that far, tantalizing country that was so often shrouded in haze.

Tom listened, enthralled, to the tales his friend told of his adventures on foot, and the wonderful things he had discovered.

There were the ancient workings which proved that gold had been mined in that part of Africa hundreds, perhaps thousands of years before the coming of the white man. Will spoke of these ancient workings at first hand, having come across several on his wanderings.

'I've seen Native women wearing solid gold ornaments round their necks and arms, but they will never say where the raw gold was discovered, or how it was smelted and fashioned,' Will said. 'Our diggers today look for gold in the rivers because that's where it has always been found in Australia and America—alluvial gold. But have you wondered where the gold we're finding in the creeks and rivers here comes from, Tom? They say it has been washed down into the river-beds through the ages. But *where* has it been washed down from? When I stake my claim it will be on Theta Hill. I believe that's where the gold now being found in the creeks originated.'

He taught Tom to use his senses more keenly than he had ever done, for Will Scully was a born poet and saw and heard with the awareness of one. They would often sit in silence for long periods just looking about them and listening to small sounds.

And on one such day they heard the sound of hoofs on dry veld and looked up to see nine splendid elands descending the side of the hill and coming directly to the spot where they sat motionless, watching. When they were within about eighty yards they suddenly froze, sensing danger. The leader was an immense bull, a magnificent creature, and they were all as sleek as stall-fed cattle. With a sudden toss of his head the leader broke the spell and they galloped off, passing within less than fifty yards of the two who watched.

'When all this is over, and the diggers have scattered to other rich fields, or have died, they'll leave this tiny piece of Africa forever American and Australian,' Will said one day.

'How do you mean?'

'Where else in Africa are krantzes, spruits and dongas called anything else? Only here, in the Eastern Transvaal, is a spruit called a creek when there's water in it, a gulch when it's dry. Only here do you find krantzes called ridges and dongas called gullies. And look at the names they've bestowed around here, Tom. Sacramento Creek, Brown's Hill, Columbia Hill, Klondyke and Duke's Hill, Peach Tree Creek and Pilgrim's Creek. This place is unique in every way—and it will remain so.'

Sometimes on a Sunday Tom and Will would climb out of the valley leading Kangaroo Joe's mule, and shoot for the pot, returning with their kill strapped to the mule's back.

Life in the valley had settled down into a happy routine, with the unexpected frequently bringing the high drama of sudden wealth or failure to the gamblers who played the alluvial gold game as others played roulette.

Andrew Howes could now walk as far as the river's edge and watch the exciting clean-up at the end of the day. When he actually held in his hand the first sizeable nugget Tom found on their claim it was as though he took a great stride forward to new health and strength. Here was tangible promise of the security he longed for before everything else, for his family and himself.

They had made many friends among the hard-working diggers, and the Russell sisters and other women of Pilgrim's Rest usually strolled along on a Sunday to drink tea or coffee, and eat the delicious rusks and cakes Katie continued to bake for Mutwa to deliver twice weekly to Pilgrim's Rest.

They were a particularly happy community, and the fact that

they were working one of the richest diggings in the world certainly helped to keep their hopes and spirits high.

Now and then rumours of impeding war would blow like a cold wind through the valley, and the people would realize what an isolated band they were, and how grossly outnumbered by the warriors of Secucuni.

It was usually newcomers from the capital who stirred up apprehension among the diggers. The authorities in Pretoria were convinced that war was inevitable with the Bapedi, which indeed later proved to be all too true.

Secucuniland was dangerously near the diggings, and although the Bapedi warriors never interfered with the diggers, now and then the camp became jittery, and occasionally they went so far as to talk of organizing a volunteer division, and a vigilance committee. But somehow it all ended in talk and nothing was done. It was easier, and pleasanter, to live for the day and let the morrow fare for itself.

16

A Christmas to Remember

The trouble with alluvial gold was that, in the phrase the diggers have given the English language, it was apt to be a 'flash in the pan'. No one could say how long his good—or his bad—fortune would last. One day a digger would be picking up nuggets on his claim like cherries from a cake, or he would roll a great boulder from its age-old bed and a cache of nuggets would be uncovered.

And that might be all his claim would yield. He might continue to toil with crow-bar, pick and spade, and hopefully pan the dirt left in his sluice-box at the end of each day. And there would be nothing more. The lucky 'lead' would have dried up completely.

So he would stake another claim, and perhaps find a fortune—or nothing at all. It was all a stupendous game of chance.

The wise ones got out when their winnings were high. Like the four men who worked three shallow claims and, before clearing out, authorized the Bank Manager to announce that they had taken £35,000 worth of gold out of Pilgrim's Creek. There were three partners, Barrington, Osborne and Farley, who cleaned up thirteen pounds eight ounces of gold, mostly in nuggets, in a single day's working. And there were the nuggets as big as rocks, some of which sent men mad.

Men would disappear overnight, taking a fortune with them. And it was estimated that more than one million pounds sterling was taken from the diggings at Pilgrim's Rest at that time.

But the work was very arduous even when the stakes were high.

About one-thousand-four-hundred diggers were working in the area, each turning over two or three tons of ground a day. The bed of the once-lovely creek and the Blyde River looked as though it had been blasted with high explosives. Every square foot of earth was being excavated and the large boulders unbedded and rolled down the banks or piled in walls on either side of the water-course.

Altogether they performed a miracle of toil and brilliant engineering, for no explosives were used, nor any tools save crow-bar, pick and shovel—and the horny hands of the diggers.

There were large boulders a-plenty on Kangaroo Joe's claim, but they were nothing compared with those on the next claim which Tom was working with the help and advice of his friend, and with Samantha's gallant aid.

When one of these gigantic boulders had to be dislodged, a hole was dug beside it and the ground loosened underneath so that the great stone could be rolled out of its 'bed'.

When these preparations had been made, Tom or Kangaroo Joe would climb onto the boulder and stand balanced on top with bare feet firmly planted. The first tremor of movement would be felt by his naked feet and with a warning shout to those work-ing below to '*Jump Clear*', he would leap to safety before the boulder lurched over into the new cradle that had been dug for it. These great rocks sometimes weighed one or two tons or even more, and most of the serious accidents at the diggings occurred when diggers mistimed their leap and were crushed under the moving boulder.

One hot November day Tom had just leapt to safety and seen the boulder he had 'ridden' roll into its new position, when a cheer from the bank made him look up.

'Chris!' he shouted. 'But this is great.'

Christian le Roux was standing with Mr. and Mrs. Howes, and his expression was a mixture of amazement and delight.

Samantha was the first to reach him as he climbed down into the dry river-bed. But this time he didn't sweep her into his arms for a bear hug, but merely took her work-roughened, dirty hand in his.

'So—you're a digger now, Samantha?' he said. And then, softly, 'Brave girl.'

To her confusion Sam found herself blushing, and for the first time in many weeks, she was conscious of the figure she cut in her faded shirt and trousers, with her bare feet and sunburnt face—for who could possibly remember to wear a kappie all the time when absorbed in the work on the diggings?

'I never thought to see anything like this,' Chris was saying when Tom joined them and wrung his hand. 'You diggers are literally tearing the world apart. Dan Viljoen told me what to expect. So did President Burgers. But no one can believe this until he's seen it with his own eyes. It's incredible!'

'It will heal, Chris,' Polly Howes told him. 'No matter what man does, Nature heals the wounds.'

'You may be right. One can hope so. But I admit I'm so amazed by what I'm seeing that I can't think of anything else. That circus act you were doing just now, Tom. You could be killed. It's perilous. You know that?'

'Of course. But there's no other way to move the boulders from the river-bed, Chris. Anyway, you've come in time to see the next part of the act. The really exciting part. Have you found anything, Kangaroo? Come, Chris, we must search the bed where that boulder was lying.'

Tom turned and ran to where Kangaroo Joe was working the bed over. He held up a small nugget, and tossed it to Andrew Howes, then went on with the search, while Samantha and Tom worked with him, and Chris watched, fascinated.

Suddenly there was a shout from Tom. The nugget he dug out with his bare hands was the shape and size of an ostrich egg. Polly and Andrew Howes had joined them, and the find was passed from one pair of cupped hands to the next. No one was more excited than Chris le Roux. His eyes shone as he judged the weight of the treasure.

'Man, this is really something I had to see for myself, to believe!' he declared. 'Now I know what you people see in this game of chance. This lump of solid gold—who would have believed it possible?'

Samantha laughed and her eyes were gently mocking.

'Oh, Chris, didn't I warn you? You're going down with gold-fever. And you're not even struggling!'

Andrew Howes always helped at the clean-up at the end of the day, and worked on the claim as his returning strength would allow. But the frustration of his long convalescence had changed him in many ways. He no longer saw himself as a digger. Nor did he feel this feverish way of life could give him real satisfaction for long. Gold he needed, and it was piling up in the bank against the future. But there were times when he found himself longing for the life of the city, as his wife did, and when his old profession called him.

That day they all watched as pan after pan of 'pay dirt' was shovelled from the sluice-box and rocked until only the gold remained gleaming in the bottom of the black iron pans. And it was a particularly good day for both claims.

Chris was impressed by the skill with which Samantha and Tom handled their pans.

'You've made a grand job of training these two diggers of

yours, Kangaroo Joe,' he said, when at last the work was done and they were tidying up before calling it a day. 'They're like old hands already.'

'As good as any on these diggings,' Kangaroo Joe said with pride. 'Given another twenty years or so an' they'll lick me at my job, shouldn't wonder.'

Samantha slipped away while the men were still talking and taking stock of the day's findings.

'There's hot water in your tent, Samantha,' her mother said when Sam joined her to help prepare the evening meal. 'You go and freshen up, dear. Put on your pink gingham frock for a change.'

'Oh, Mama, you're a darling!' There was a world of understanding in the look that passed between mother and daughter.

After the meal they turned out the lamps and took their chairs outside, settling down to talk. It had showered several times during the day and a multitude of flying ants and other insects had been attracted by the lamplight and invaded the marquee.

It was beautiful in the moonlight, and the night hid much of the ugliness which men had wreaked in the valley. One's eyes were drawn to the magnificent heads of the mountains against the star-jewelled sky, and the lamps that glowed in the tents scattered up and down the valley. There were moving lights, too, where men carrying lanterns followed the winding footpaths, as they made their way to the tents of friends, to the brightly lit pubs, and the canvas billiard-room recently set up on the edge of the market square.

Chris had brought back the wagon and team which Andrew Howes had lent Dan Viljoen, and had left it at the farm before riding over to Pilgrim's Rest.

'Anna Viljoen is my father's cousin,' he explained. 'They called in at my farm in passing and explained all that had happened to you, and we then arranged that I would drive your wagon back when the oxen had rested.'

'We will never forget their kindness to us,' Polly Howes said warmly.

'Nor will they forget all you did for them. Tante Anna told me about the gown.'

'It was so little to do.'

'Not to her, believe me. And now tell me, do you intend to remain here at Pilgrim's Rest, my friends?'

Andrew Howes looked across at his wife and she nodded and smiled.

'For the present, yes, Chris,' Andrew Howes said. 'As you see we are making a good deal of money here, and whatever our future plans may be, that is most necessary.'

'And the farm?'

'You know the story of how we came into possession of it. The understanding is that if Dan Viljoen wants it back, it is his.'

Chris laughed.

'That is not his story. The farm is truly yours. That is why I'd like to know if you plan to work it in the near future?'

'The near future? No, Chris. I know no more about farming than I did about gold-mining. We became very fond of Morenson. It's a beautiful farm as you know. At present Mutwa and Katie are doing their best with it.'

'Then perhaps you'd consider my proposal.' Chris sat forward the better to study his friend's face. 'I'd like to use Morenson—for a time at any rate. I'd like to hunt in this region during the summer months, and use it to store the hides and horns as Dan did in the past. I'd also like to try and develop the lands. They look good to me. I believe your neighbour, Tom McLachlan, is farming successfully.'

'That could work out very well, Chris. Mutwa and Katie would remain on there, of course, and continue to bring us supplies of food for our use and to sell here.'

'Of course. But no farm improves by being left unworked.'

'Oh, Chris,' Samantha teased. 'How transparent you are! Be honest and admit that it isn't farming or hunting that is the attraction.'

'And what do you think it is, Samantha?' Chris's eyes locked with hers in the soft light.

'Why—' She was suddenly embarrassed. 'Why, it's the gold, of course,' she said breathlessly. 'You'll be the next one for Kangaroo Joe to put through his paces.'

Kangaroo Joe was always ready to 'doss down' as soon as the evening meal was over. Now he stood up and stretched, yawning prodigiously.

'Makes sense at that,' he said. 'It's wrong for a powerful young chap like you to waste y'strength mucking about on a farm. Think it over. 'Night, folks.' And he was off down the track to his tent, leaving a trail of evil-smelling tobacco smoke behind him.

Before Chris rode off the next morning he had a long talk with Polly and Andrew Howes.

'If you mean to stay here through the summer at least, you

should have something more permanent than these tents,' he said. 'Summer storms are violent in this part of the world, you know. Let me run up a house for you.'

'Oh, Chris, you make it sound so easy. Run up a house, indeed! As though I were running up a dress,' Polly Howes laughed.

'No really, it would be quite simple,' he insisted. 'These "boys" I've brought over with me from my farm are used to building. Together we built my homestead and all the outbuildings. I could get the materials from Lydenburg and do the job before getting started on the farm. Just say the word.'

'The word is "*Wonderful!*"' Andrew Howes said. 'I've been worried about life under canvas with the summer months upon us. And I think I'd be of more use helping with the lighter building jobs, than down on the claim. That work is still rather much for me.'

'Fine, then I'll go ahead. I was looking at the three houses that have already gone up. You choose your site, and I'll bring my "boys" over to clear and level the ground while I'm away in Lydenburg.'

The houses, like the tent shops and shacks, faced onto the dirt road running parallel to the river, but sufficiently high above it to be in no danger should summer storms bring Pilgrim's Creek and mountain rivulets down in flood.

They were the usual type of Colonial house, built of corrugated iron and wood, with large rooms, a wide stoep on two or three sides of the house, and an iron roof.

By the greatest good fortune Chris was spared the hazardous trip to Lydenburg. Major MacDonald heard of the intended house-building, as he heard of everything that was happening in the district, and he rode over at once to stop Chris from starting on his journey.

'Rhodes was about to build a house for himself at Mac Mac,' he said. 'He'd bought all the materials and they're still on his wagon as they were loaded at Lydenburg. He's decided now not to go ahead with his plans. Has his own good reasons, no doubt, and no questions asked. But I happen to know that if you were to make him a reasonable offer for the stuff, it would be yours.'

And so work went right ahead with the house. The steep ground was levelled, with six steps leading down to the road, and the banks built up against storm-water damage with boulders from the creek.

Polly Howes was overjoyed, and her husband was kept busy doing work which did not put too great a strain on him.

'We'll have it up by Christmas,' Chris promised.

And, by sheer hard work and the willing help of neighbours, he kept his word. When a job of building had to be done at Pilgrim's Rest it was everyone's concern, and there were always willing volunteers ready to give their labour and skill after digging hours, and during week-ends.

While the work of door and window fitting and painting was still going on, a wagon stopped at the gate one day, and the driver handed Polly Howes a letter from Mrs. McLachlan. The two women had become friends, although they were both kept so busy that they could seldom arrange a meeting.

'Dear Polly,' she wrote. 'Tom tells me that the time has come for work to begin on your garden. So I'm sending you Jacob, my gardener, who is a wizard with green fingers, his two helpers, and the "makings" of a garden. May it brighten your valley home and bring you colour and fragrance.'

There were sacks of kraal manure and other sacks full of lawn grass roots, dahlia and iris bulbs, rose bushes, shrubs and seedlings, and golden privet for a hedge.

Polly Howes was so moved that she wept with joy—before rolling up her sleeves, tying on a flour-sack apron which she kept for rough work, and tackling the work that was so close to her heart, with Jacob and his two helpers in charge of the major operation of laying out the garden and planting the lawns.

'You may count yourselves lucky if you get bread and jam from now on,' she informed her family. 'I'm staking *my* claim in a garden.'

With the bread and pies, roast joints and chickens which Katie sent regularly twice a week, there was no possibility of the family enduring a famine.

Richard Somers and Will Scully were frequent visitors and were always made most welcome and pressed to stay for a meal. But a certain coolness had developed between Chris and Richard which surprised everyone except Polly Howes.

'Mama, they're both such dears,' Samantha said one night

when her mother had come into Sam's tent to say good night. 'I expected them to be great friends. Is it because Richard is so very English, and Chris so proud of being a South African with a Boer father?'

Her mother laughed.

'Oh, Samantha, don't you really know what makes them spar? It's you, my darling daughter! They may not even know it themselves yet, although they probably do. But it's that old green-eyed monster that's bedevilling them. Ignore it, and treat each of them as the good friend he is. It will sort itself out in the end. You're not to worry.'

Samantha was so surprised that she was speechless, and her mother left her lying in bed wide-eyed as she digested the astonishing news her mother had given her.

The Australian diggers who had employed Will Scully had struck a bad patch and had been obliged to dispense with his services for they could not even afford to feed him. But Will was taken on immediately by another group of Australians whose luck was in. They paid him the standard wage of one ounce of gold—then worth £3.10*s*. 0*d*.—a week, without food.

He saved every penny he could, and earned money on the side by making tents in his spare time. With his first earnings he had bought some double-width unbleached calico and a palm and needle. And with these he made his first tent. The cost of the material was about seventeen shillings, and he completed the work in five evenings. When he had been living in his tent for ten days a 'new chum' bought it over his head for £1.15*s*.0*d*.

Will Scully at once recognized the possibility of earning extra money in this way, and he soon became known as 'that chap who always has a tent to sell'. Whenever he sold a new tent he would move in with Tom along with his few possessions, and busily make yet another calico tent. He was repeatedly invited to make his home with the family, but his independent spirit made him refuse.

As Christmas approached so the work on the house and garden became even more frenzied. Even before the paint was properly dry in the rooms, furniture was moved into place which Mutwa brought over from Morenson. Pretty floral cretonne was bought and Samantha helped her mother sew curtains, hanging wardrobes, and cushion-covers far into the night.

Kangaroo Joe laughed at the idea that he would move in with them.

'Give me canvas every time, ma'am,' he said, when Polly Howes pressed him to make a room in the house his own. 'T'ain't healthy living cooped up between walls with a tin roof overhead. Give me my tent every time, or the open sky. That way I'm safe from draughts and suffocation.'

'Have it your own way, my friend. But at least you must continue to share our meals.'

Kangaroo Joe spat tobacco juice at a lizard and, Polly Howes was pleased to note, missed his target.

'If it's all the same to you, ma'am,' he said, 'I'd rather eat in my tent. No offence meant, y'understand. It's jest—waal, sittin' at table riles me, and upsets the digestion.'

'I understand,' Polly smiled, and her glance could not help straying to his beloved hat. 'As soon as we move into our house Katie will be with us. Your meals will be sent over to you, Kangaroo Joe.'

'Thank you kindly. I've never ate so good in all my days I do assure you.'

What a Christmas it turned out to be. One which none of them would ever be likely to forget.

It seemed at times during the day that almost everyone in the valley was taking advantage of the general invitation to share a glass of good cheer and 'bless the house'. Polly Howes, Katie and Samantha were run off their feet between kitchen and living-room, replenishing the platters of sliced cold meats and chickens, the boerewors and salads, the mince pies, Christmas puddings and fruit-cake, the nuts and the sweets, the wine and the beer.

The day was far too hot for anything but cold food, fortunately, and of this there was plenty.

There had been a braaivleis in the market square the night before, with dancing on a bucksail floor to the music of fiddles, concertinas and mandolins. And if it was largely a 'bull' dance because of the scarcity of womenfolk, everyone enjoyed the romp immensely, and the ladies were escorted home before the time when fists, bottles and pick handles began to fly.

Samantha had worn the filigree gold brooch Richard Somers had given her to pin the white chiffon fissue of her new blue gown, and a pearl necklace that had once been the proud possession of Christian le Roux's grandmother when she was a girl.

Had her mother not given her a clue, the behaviour of the two young men would have puzzled and hurt her. As it was, Samantha handled the delicate situation with understanding, and a maturity that surprised her mother and set her mind at rest.

Girls, as well as boys, matured very early in this new land because of the hard conditions, and the responsibilities they had to assume.

What did surprise and pain Samantha was that, for the first time in her life, Tom had rebuffed her when she would have talked to him about the complications that had arisen in her relationship with the two young men. She had always turned naturally to him, and talked freely when faced with a difficult situation. But Tom had reacted strangely. Almost, Sam thought in bewilderment, as though he were jealous of Chris and Richard.

Storm-clouds built up all through the afternoon on Christmas Day, and a terrible storm broke over the valley in early evening. The mounting roar of the creek filled the diggers with concern for their claims, and those whose tents were pitched too near the banks hastily moved to higher sites, or stored their possessions in safety and spent the night with friends.

Will Scully shared Tom's room, and early the next morning the two friends set out to climb Theta Hill.

'The creek's coming down in spate so there's nothing we can do on the claims today,' Tom said at breakfast. 'If the water subsides by tomorrow we'll have to work flat out to repair the damage and build a new water race. Let's make the most of it and stretch our legs today, Will.'

The Russell sisters had brought over a basket of ripe peaches when they called on Christmas Day, for their claim was on Peach Tree Creek where the peaches were the first in the valley to ripen. Tom and Will filled their pockets with the yellow cling-stone peaches before setting out.

When Andrew Howes had gone out onto the front stoep very early that morning to look at the weather, he had found Kangaroo Joe rolled up on the wooden floor snoring lustily. The fact that both the floor and his blanket were wet had made no difference, and he only snorted when Polly Howes scolded him for not sleeping in a dry bed indoors.

'Rain never gave me a cold in my life,' he declared. 'You work up a good body steam when you're dossing down in wet clothes. Had to bring my tent and clobber up, though, or they'd have been washed away when the creek rose.'

Nobody made any comment when a fit of sneezing caught him unawares and his pipe shot out of his mouth and had to be retrieved from the garden bed below the stoep, and wiped clean of mud on the sleeve of his flannel shirt.

But Polly Howes saw to it that he ate a hearty breakfast, and she had his blanket whisked away, washed, and out on the clothesline in the sunshine before he knew what was going on.

It had been arranged weeks before that a football match would be held on the afternoon of Boxing Day, and everyone watched and measured the strength of the sun, betting on the chances of the Market Square 'field' drying out in time.

The match was to be played between Home-born versus Colonists, the home team including many ex-public schoolboys from good English families who had been sent out to South Africa in the hope that they would 'settle down'. They were mostly boys between the ages of eighteen and twenty, and included three from Rugby, four from Eton, four Harrovians, two Cheltonians, one from Uppingham and two from Clifton.

'We'll be back in time for the match,' Tom called to his aunt from the gate, as he and Will set off.

'If you're not home for dinner at one o'clock I'll save it for you,' she promised. 'How you'll climb those muddy slopes I can't imagine.'

They were perhaps two-thirds of the way to the top of Theta Hill when Will exclaimed and bent to pick something up from among the grass roots which the storm water had exposed.

'Look at this, Tom!' he cried. 'A perfect golden feather! Did you ever see anything prettier?'

'Good heavens! That bears out what you said about the gold in the creek having been originally washed down from Theta.'

'Of course it does. And, to my knowledge, this isn't the first nugget that's been picked up on these slopes after rain. Tell you what, Tom. I'm going to stake a claim right here. I've managed to save a few pounds, enough to buy necessities and feed myself for a spell. First thing in the morning I'm giving notice to the Aussies I'm working for, and walking over to Mac Mac to stake this claim. Here, help me mark it off, will you? We'll pin-point the spot where I picked up this nugget right in the dead centre of my claim—for luck. Meanwhile, keep it under your hat, Tom. If word gets round that I've found this nugget the others will come swarming.'

'Good luck to you, Will. May it bring you a fortune,' Tom said with feeling.

Although the Market Square was a quagmire in places, this in no way dampened the enthusiasm of players or spectators that afternoon. Even before play commenced several fights had to be broken up, for feelings ran high between the rival factions.

Rugby rules were observed, with a few novel innovations introduced as the game progressed, and the Home-born team received a severe beating although they did manage to secure one goal and several touch-downs against their tough adversaries.

'A very different kettle of fish it would have been, I'm telling you, had the Home-borns had a few good Welshmen to back them up and put some spunk into their game,' Taffy Jones lamented. 'A pity it is that Wales couldn't save them from this disgrace.'

'It was the tragic shortage of Irishmen that brought about the shameful defeat, I'll be telling you, my good man,' Paddy Maloney cried. 'Welshmen, indeed! Little bandy-legged fellers who couldn't catch a pig if they tried.'

A pretty fight ensued during which both Wales and Ireland rolled in the mud.

'I think this is where we make for home, dear,' Andrew Howes suggested mildly. 'Before the real fun begins, as it were.'

It had certainly been a Christmas to remember, even though everyone was glad enough to get back to 'porridge and working togs' the next day, with the sun shining brightly on the scene of storm havoc, and a tremendous job of reclamation to be tackled.

17

A Dangerous Mission

The worst electric storm in living memory broke over Pilgrim's Rest on New Year's Eve. Lightning rent the dark skies and cracked whips of fire over the heads of the mountains, and thunder shook the earth.

The tent settlement was reduced to insignificance by the magnitude of the storm's fury. And when the rain began to fall it was as though the heavens had opened, and a deluge poured down old and new water-courses scarring the mountains and valleys. The Blyde River was transformed into a churning brown torrent within minutes of the first downpour.

'What a way to begin a new year!' Samantha shouted above the din of the storm. The house echoed with the wild drumming of rain on the corrugated iron roof, and the savage roar of thunder. 'Let's hope it isn't a warning of what we can expect in 1874!'

As they were soon to find out, it might well have been. For it was to prove a year of high drama and great change, involving every one of them before the sensational twelve months were spent.

To begin with, the relative harmony of the diggings was threatened by unruly newcomers, and Major MacDonald found it necessary to move his office from Mac Mac to Pilgrim's Rest in order to exert firmer control.

He was a splendid man for a particularly tough job. All the old diggers liked and respected him, and he was usually strong enough to control the rowdy element that was tramping and riding in over the hills from far and near. Deserters from the army or from ships that had called at South African ports; criminals on the run who sought to lose themselves in the hurly-burly of the mining camp; the wild Black Sheep whose families were only too thankful to pay them a regular remittance on condition that they stayed away from their respectable homes—the lust for gold drew them all like a magnet.

Nor was it only the gold that attracted them. There was a peculiar excitement about digging for alluvial gold that triggered off the gambling instinct that is in most of us to some extent. Life in a mining camp had many things to offer these men.

By no means all the newcomers were desperate characters hell-bent on stirring up trouble. Many were men who had footslogged hundreds of miles simply to escape the humdrum monotony of the highly respectable lives they had found it unbearable to continue. There were the restless and reckless, who were otherwise ordinary decent men.

There were scholars and scoundrels, adventurers and a few dreamers, bullies and drunkards, tough old miners, and many youngsters who, like Tom Maxwell and Will Scully, were rapidly growing to manhood in that forcing house of character.

They were an amazing collection of men, some of whom were to become legends in the land of their adoption. They came from every country in the world, and between them they spoke almost every known language. Some struck it lucky. Some did not.

It was the new arrivals at the diggings who caused the trouble whenever it flared up, as it did with increasing frequency.

Only twelve days of the new year had been ticked off when Major MacDonald thought it necessary to write to President Burgers explaining that the situation was getting out of hand. He also forwarded petitions from the diggers asking for their own representatives in the Volksraad, and nominating Tom McLachlan and F. P. Mansfield as their spokesmen.

There was great excitement in the valley when the State Secretary replied that the President would arrive at Pilgrim's Rest on the 2nd of February. He asked for the diggers to assemble there so that he could meet them, and go over their grievances with them.

But suddenly Major MacDonald was faced with an unexpectedly dangerous situation.

The wet season had set in after the deluge on New Year's Eve, and all rivers were running very high indeed. This meant that the diggers were often idle, and there was nothing for them to do but drink themselves into an ugly, suspicious frame of mind, gamble away what gold they had, fight, and talk themselves into the belief that the President was only coming to Pilgrim's Rest to 'put the screw on them' and 'interfere with their freedom'.

In no time at all they were fighting wild, and in desperation Major MacDonald sent a messenger with instructions to ride with all speed, begging President Burgers to postpone his visit until the men had quietened down.

But the President was not a man to be intimidated. Nor could he believe that the diggers would harm him when he so sincerely had their interests at heart, and had proved this time and again.

At the last moment the volatile situation was changed by the courageous action of Henry Struben, one of the first men to discover gold in the Eastern Transvaal, and a man of wealth, property, and great understanding.

The President's wagon and accompanying horsemen had arrived on the far bank of the swollen Blyde River, and a council of war was actually being held among the hundreds of diggers assembled on the Pilgrim's Rest bank of the river. Their mood was dangerous, and Major MacDonald packed a gun for the first time since taking office as Gold Commissioner. He knew that anything could happen with most serious consequences.

'Get back to Pretoria!' the furious diggers yelled. 'We can manage our own affairs in our own way, curse you! Cross the river at your peril!'

But the roar of the river drowned their threats.

All President Burgers could hear was a chorus of men's voices. All he could see at that distance, through the curtain of rain, were the upraised hands of the diggers who crowded the far bank. Not for a moment did he suspect that they were clenched fists rather than hands raised in welcome.

But Henry Struben, who accompanied the President's party, and on whose farm Pilgrim's Rest was actually situated, was under no such delusions. He knew very well what ugly consequences could result from the President's visit. And he was determined to use his own strategy and tactics to protect the man he admired and loved.

Others in the President's party, who also understood the situation, pressed that he should at all costs be persuaded to return to Pretoria.

'Imagine what such a retreat would mean to our Government's prestige,' Henry Struben argued. 'These men must be handled in a way they will understand—and respond to.'

He conferred with the President, and was given permission to carry out his daring plan.

Stripping himself, Henry Struben braved the dangers of the swollen river. And, as soon as the diggers realized what was taking place, they cheered him on, recognizing the courage of the man, and his determination.

As he reached the far bank diggers swarmed down to help him out of the surging river, and MacDonald threw his cloak about him.

That act instantly changed the mood of the diggers from hostility to wild enthusiasm. They not only listened to what Struben had to say, but warmly applauded when he introduced himself as the owner of the property from which they were being allowed to reap their harvest of gold.

He was able to convince them without difficulty that the President was their friend, and that he had made the uncomfortable journey solely to hear their grievances and assist them.

'If you good fellows will fetch a long rope and give me your assistance, we will have the President safely across the river in no time,' he said. 'Then you can give him the warm welcome he so richly deserves. We must always remember that President Burgers has been branded by his many enemies and detractors as "The Diggers' Champion," which he is proud to be.'

Only Henry Struben was aware of the fact that the President could not swim, and he and Major MacDonald organized the dangerous task as the diggers hauled the wagon across the flooded river, with President Burgers on board.

And what a reception he received! It was hard to believe that these enthusiastic fellows had been swearing violence only an hour before, every word of which they meant.

A conference was immediately arranged at which the proposed new mining laws were discussed and accepted with minor amendments. The diggers' two representatives were unanimously voted to the Volksraad, and the men then insisted upon giving the President 'a dinner he'd remember' in the camp.

How could the President ever hope to forget the banquet held in his honour? Mathias Mockett, always referred to as 'the Bos'n' because of the years he had spent before the mast in his young days, was in charge of the catering.

Heroically, the President and his party tackled the heaped plates of food that were planked down before them by the Bos'n himself. The final course was plum duff served with brandy sauce, and although the pastry 'needed a sledge-hammer to dent it', according to Kangaroo Joe, the brandy sauce was given the highest praise.

Fortunately for all concerned, the rains stopped, the rivers subsided, and the President and his men were given a great send-off while the congenial mood prevailed.

But it was by no means the end of Major MacDonald's problems, and several times, in the riotous months ahead, he declared his intention of throwing in the sponge and clearing out.

No matter how hard he worked, all Will Scully's efforts to strike gold on Theta Hill met with failure. His claim was either washed out by heavy rains or he lacked sufficient water to wash his pay-dirt. Nothing he did worked out for his enrichment. Now and then he would find a small nugget, but never anything to cause optimism or relieve his poverty.

He collected rubies and garnets, not for their worth, but simply because he enjoyed the fire they held, and these he stored in a tin which had contained Blakey's metal boot tips.

Kangaroo Joe was becoming strangely restless and moody. He

would sit alone for hours when work on the claim was over, smoking his pipe and staring into the distance, resenting intrusion.

He had salted away a fortune for the first time in his life, and instead of this giving him a sense of security, it only unsettled him.

Once he tried to explain to Tom how he felt about it, for Tom was closer to him than anyone.

'Seems like the end of the trail when everything's fixed up an' tidy-like,' he said. 'It don't mean a doggone thing to me, all that dough don't that's stashed away. Far's I'm concerned, the Bank Manager can have it and welcome. Like I always say, Tom, it's the fossicking that's the thing. Finding gold. Working a claim yer own way. Sweating yer guts out, who cares? But that's the life, boy. This here claim of mine's jest about worked out. Do I care? Never on yer sweet life I don't. My feet's itching, Tom. My shoulders are weary fer the feel of my swag. I'm sick an' tired of bein' buried alive in this here hole of a valley. Only place you can look far at is *up*. And who in hell wants to look at the blooming sky all the time?'

'Any other place in mind, Kangaroo Joe?' Tom asked, giving no indication of the sadness he felt at the thought that they might be coming to a parting of the ways.

'Nope. But I'm keeping an ear to the ground, Tom. Somethin' tells me I'll be hitting out before too long. Where to? Can't say right now. But I'll know the call when it comes—an' I'll let you know.'

Chris rode over from the farm quite often, and he enjoyed lending a hand on the claims at such times. He was interested in gold-mining, and delighted when they struck it rich, but the gold bug hadn't really bitten him. He was still a man of the land, and always would be. A sower and reaper. A man who loved trees and the gold of wheat infinitely more than mineral wealth.

'I can see what the President means when he says we need this gold if the Transvaal's to be saved,' he said one evening in May when they were all sitting round the living-room fire after dinner. 'But what's happening to the gold that's being taken from this valley? You know as well as I do. It's going out of the country, legally and illegally. At all events it certainly isn't benefiting the Transvaal Republic as it should do. There should be stricter controls.'

'So you're concerned about the rumours we've heard that the Transvaal is practically bankrupt?' Andrew Howes heaped logs on the fire then turned to study Christian le Roux's face.

'Rumours? Would to God they were no more than that. Every Transvaaler knows that our State is bankrupt. That it owes the Cape Commercial Bank alone £60,000 at this moment, and has scarcely sufficient funds to meet the salaries of its public servants. We all know that the old "bluebacks" are being called in, but we also know that the new note issue is hardly more popular. What have we got to back it with? You know what happened when the President gave MacDonald £1,000 in bluebacks with which to buy gold. The diggers refused to accept the paper currency, didn't they? They'd only part with their gold for coins. And who can blame them? The President's up against the Volksraad in this. They refuse to believe that we must have our own coinage, as every other country has theirs.'

'And this talk about making war on Secucuni, Chris? The rumours are too persistent for there to be no truth in them.'

'Yes, the rumours are growing, aren't they? But where's the money to come from to pay for such a war? We know that the Bapedi have been stealing our cattle for years, and that Secucuni refuses to pay the hut tax our Government is trying to impose on his people. But how can we wage war without money or arms? And if we did fight, what good would such a war do? We need peace in our land, not war. There's been too much bloodshed as it is. That's the way I see it, anyway.'

'I find it hard to believe that Mr. Burgers favours war,' Andrew Howes said. 'He's essentially a man of peace.'

'I agree. But is he strong enough to hold it off? My father, who knows him very well, has told me how much pressure is being used against the President on many issues. How long will it be before he's forced to give way?'

Their questions were soon to be answered by President Burgers himself. For in June he again visited Pilgrim's Rest.

This time he accepted Andrew Howes's invitation to stay with them, and there was not a member of the family who wasn't won over by his natural charm and sincere goodness.

Two important missions had brought him back to the diggings. The first was to buy a quantity of gold from which a token number of sovereigns were to be struck at the Royal Mint in London. This was a victory for the President, and his acquisition of the gold for these coins was to be resolved in a remarkable way.

A few years before, a man named Potgieter had been a member of the President's former congregation at Hanover in the Cape Province. This man had been devoted to the then Dominee Burgers, and had followed him with his family when he moved to the Transvaal.

When Potgieter wanted to try his fortune on the diggings, it had been the President who had helped fit him out for the venture.

Potgieter had pegged several claims at Pilgrim's Rest and worked hard to make a living. But luck was against him. Finally he had to admit defeat.

It was on the very day of the President's visit to the valley that Potgieter loaded his family and all his possessions on to his wagon for their return to Pretoria.

The oxen were inspanned and everything was in readiness for the journey when Potgieter decided to go down to the creek for a last time and 'to say farewell to my claim'.

He was turning to leave the scene of his bitter failure when he noticed a crack in a large boulder which he had not seen before. Acting impulsively, for his family and the oxen were getting restive, he brushed the sand out of the crack and inspected it more closely.

It was only then that he saw the unmistakable colour of gold, and two large nuggets were revealed which were to change his fortune. He called them the 'Emma' and the 'Adelina', and they weighed 16½ ounces and 22 ounces 17½ dwts respectively.

These nuggets were bought by President Burgers, and provided the actual gold used to mint the famous 837 sovereigns, around which such storms were to rage.

President Burgers' second reason for visiting Pilgrim's Rest was even more startling.

He had come, he explained, to recruit an Uitlander Commando of twenty-five volunteers. These men were required to set out for Delagoa Bay to convoy a vital shipment of arms and ammunition to Pretoria. They would be well paid, for it was appreciated that the mission was a perilous one.

With the exception of ten tons of gunpowder, which had been purchased from the firm of Pigou and Wilkes, this war material was a gift to the Transvaal Republic from the German Government. It was, in fact, part of the loot seized during the Franco-German War.

It was only during the winter months, from June to September, that men could venture into the Lowveld with any degree of safety. The risk to man and beast was much less then than in summer, when fever and the dreaded tsetse fly killed men and the oxen that drew their wagons.

'I shall speak frankly to you,' the President told the assembled diggers when he addressed them in the Market Square. 'The war we have dreaded for so long can no longer be averted. Secucuni is preparing to strike—and we must be ready to defend ourselves against his warriors. It is of vital importance that we arm ourselves. In the capital we are training our men—Boer and Uitlander alike—and we call upon you diggers to play your part in an expedition of the utmost importance.

'Major MacDonald, late of the American Army, and a man you have all learned to trust, has agreed to lead the expedition. Twenty-five men are wanted. They will be taking their lives in their hands, but everything possible will be done to ensure their safe return. And payment will be high.

'We have received word that a shipment of arms and ammunition has arrived at Delagoa Bay. The expedition will be required to set out without loss of time, for it may well take the whole of winter before the mission is fully accomplished.

'I want every volunteer to be fully alive to the dangers he may have to face. Last year, as you probably know, thirty-five men braved the Lowveld for various reasons. Of these twenty-seven died of fever. Those who died had ventured there either too early or too late in the season for any real margin of safety. We will not make that mistake.

'We want lean, wiry men rather than those of powerful physique, because it has been proved that such men withstand fever better than do robust men.

'I do not want you to pledge yourselves immediately. Sleep on it, men. And in the morning those of you who are willing to undertake this venture into the Lowveld should hand in your names to

Major MacDonald, whom I now name as leader of the expedition, and to whom every man must swear obedience.'

Had President Burgers been prepared to accept recruits on the spot, more than half the camp would have signed up in a fever of enthusiasm. But he was coming to know the men more realistically. And he understood how grave the consequences could well be should a party of blow-hot-blow-cold recruits set out to face the dangers and trials of the mission ahead.

The fire was back in Kangaroo Joe's blue eyes. His step was light and his shoulders squared.

'This here's what I've been waiting for, Tom lad,' he declared, thumping his friend on the back. 'A chance to stretch my blooming legs—to squint as far as my blooming eyes can see—and beyond. This is what was in the wind when I told you I could smell something good coming up. Tom, if my name ain't first on the Major's list come morning, I'll eat my hat!'

Will Scully joined the family round the table that night. He was unusually silent and appeared to have lost his appetite. But his eyes, too, had a fire kindled in them. Tom had seen it before many times when they had been alone in the mountains and Will had opened his heart to his friend.

It had been there at other times when Will had gazed across the hazy Lowveld that seemed to be a world away below their high escarpment, instead of the three to four thousand feet it was in actual fact.

'Can't you see it as it was thousands of years ago, Tom?' Will had said on one such day. 'With the ocean washing right up to these cliffs. When this great escarpment was the coastline of our continent—the oldest continent in the world? Sometimes I can actually hear the waves crashing against those cliffs. I can see the white crests foaming and breaking. I can hear the cries of the seabirds of those early days. When we venture into the Lowveld we'll be walking on the ocean bed. Think of it, Tom! Just think. What caused the seas to recede? What forced the waters back to the coastline they now accept? Sometimes I can smell salt in the air. And when fever-mists cover the Lowveld, as they do so often, isn't it easy to imagine that it's the sea rising and falling, swelling and breaking, just as it was all those years ago?'

So Tom was prepared when Will said, 'This is what I've been waiting for, Tom. This is my chance.'

'To walk on the floor of the ocean?'

'Just that. And more, to see the new life that's taken over in the years between. The mineral, vegetable and animal life. It's almost too good to be true, isn't it?'

'Yes,' Tom said. 'I'd say yes, it is, Will.'

As was the custom they sat round the living-room fire that night. Chris had ridden in to attend the meeting in the Market Square. He, too, had been unusually silent during the meal.

'Well,' Thomas Burgers said. 'What do you think our chances are? Will I get my twenty-five men?'

It was Chris who answered.

'You'll get them all right, Meneer President. Had you enlisted them after your meeting the men of this valley would have signed up as one man. Oh, you'll get them all right. And so I can say without feeling in any way a traitor to your cause that my name will not be among those who sign up.'

'Your reasons are your own, Christian.'

'Of course. That I know. But I would like to explain them if you will hear me out. I am a Boer, like yourself.' He caught Samantha's eye, smiled, and corrected, 'By birth I am half Boer, half Uitlander. A good mixture of blood. But first of all I am a farmer. If my country is threatened I will naturally take up arms and fight for it. What man would not? If I felt it my duty I would venture down into the Lowveld without question. But in my heart I'm not sure about the rights and wrongs of this war against Secucuni and his warriors, that's in the wind. My reason insists there are other ways of dealing with this matter of cattle rustling and the levying of hut taxes. That's all. But I wanted you to know how I feel about it.'

'There was no need for you to tell me, Christian le Roux. I not only understand how you feel, I confess that some of your doubts also trouble me.' President Burgers's face reflected a deeply troubled mind. 'But you must believe me when I say that I am doing what I sincerely feel I have to do. Pray God there will be no need for war. But it is perhaps better—no, it is indeed better—that we should be prepared for the worst.'

'Major MacDonald's a brave man, and the best you could

possibly have found for this difficult task,' Andrew Howes said.

'And he will gather the right men round him.'

'I hope you're right, President Burgers,' Will Scully said. 'Because, if he'll accept me, I'm going to be one of those men. My reasons for going are entirely selfish. But I'll honour my word, sir.'

The President studied Will Scully with searching, knowing eyes.

'You're young, but you're made of the right stuff, Will Scully. I wish you—good luck.'

Kangaroo Joe had pushed open the door and joined them, after returning his plate and 'eating irons', as he called them, to their place in the kitchen.

'So you're joining up, are you, young Will?' he said. 'Good for you, lad. But I've sworn my name will be first on the list, and first it'll be. I'm no patriot, Mister President. It doesn't matter a row of tacks to me if we're bringing back gunpowder or cocks' feathers. It's a chance to stretch my legs. To get out o' this valley—out into the open again. Right now I'm sick to the guts with gold. Unless it's still buried under the earth that is. I'm joining up because it's what I want to do. That's how it is. Thought you ought to know, p'haps.'

President Burgers smiled at the big man who was watching him with some uneasiness. What if the truth had damned his chances? Kangaroo Joe thought. But he had felt obliged to 'come clean' with this man he respected.

'I can't think of any man better fitted for this job. Major MacDonald will be proud to have you, Kangaroo Joe.'

'Thank you, Mister President. I'll sure do what I can.'

'How interesting it is whenever we come to a show-down like this in life,' Andrew Howes observed. 'It just demonstrates every time that each man jack of us must prove himself in his own way.'

'Every woman, too,' his wife said quietly.

'I didn't think this would be the right time to talk about it, Uncle Andrew,' Tom said. 'I thought, perhaps, it would be better later on, when we were alone.'

'What's on your mind, Tom?' his uncle asked.

Tom cleared his throat. He felt his face flush and his hands were cold.

'You remember what you said to me that day in Pretoria? That I had to give this country a chance, and then decide for myself whether I wanted to make it—make it my own, or go back to England?'

'I remember very well, Tom.'

'Well—I want to make it my own. This isn't—it isn't something I've just decided. I don't want you to think that. It isn't just that I'm excited because Kangaroo Joe and Will are joining Major MacDonald's expedition—and I want to go along too. You believe that, don't you?'

'Yes, Tom.'

'Well—well, I do want to go with them—if they'll have me, that is. I'm strong. I'm a pretty good walker—thanks to Will mostly.' He flashed his friend a weak smile. 'But it's something I find it hard to explain. I want to stake a claim. That's really what it is. I want to be a South African. To feel this is my country. And it's only by staking a claim—by doing something to prove—prove *to myself*, that is—that I'll be one. So I want your permission, Uncle Andrew. May I join up?'

'How old are you, Tom?' the President asked.

'Nearly sixteen, sir. That is, sixteen in September.'

'Then it's not a question of age. Men younger than you have played their part in the history of our country. Played it nobly. During the Great Trek. In the various Kaffir Wars.' President Burgers sighed deeply. 'No, it's not a question of age. Just of preparedness. Are you prepared, Tom, for what you may have to face?'

'Forgive me, but does anyone ever know if he's prepared for what he may have to face—today or tomorrow?' Chris asked. 'I doubt it. How do we know if we're prepared—until we're tested and it's proved?'

'True.' Andrew Howes looked across at his wife, and she met his eyes steadily. 'Well, Polly?' he asked.

'Surely, as we're agreed that at fifteen—nearly sixteen—one is a man in this country, then the decision rests with Tom. As one of you—I think it was you, Andrew—said just now, every man must prove himself in his own way. If this is Tom's way—then you go with our blessing, dear boy.'

'Oh, Mama, good for you!' Samantha cried. There were unashamed tears on her cheeks. 'I was hoping you'd say that. Because, if I were a boy—'

'Yes, Samantha?' Chris asked gently. 'What would you do?'

'How can I possibly say, since I'm not a boy? But I think I'd do just what each one of you has decided to do—if I were you. And I'm not going to squeal because Kangaroo Joe and Tom are going off and leaving Papa and me with two claims to work, and—and to worry ourselves silly over them. I'm going to get on with the job. That's what we're all doing in our own way, isn't it really?'

'Andrew, you and Samantha won't have to work the claims single-handed—if you'll let me come in on this work with you,' Chris said. 'I'll arrange for Kameel to load the wagons and take them down to the coast with the other trekkers when they leave. My father, or Dan Viljoen, or some other friend can attend to the selling. They'll do it willingly. So I can stay on here through the winter—and dig for gold.'

'Fine, Chris!' Andrew Howes accepted the offer at once.

'Don't let him fool you, Papa,' Samantha laughed, but her laugh was shaky. 'He's going down with gold-fever, and hasn't the courage to admit it.' Her eyes shone as she looked at Chris.

And Tom, watching her, knew that he was indeed facing a testing time. Sam and Chris—they belonged. He must accept it like a man. He welcomed the trials and dangers of the Death Trail. It was the medicine he needed.

18

The Death Trail

As Chris had foreseen, there was certainly no difficulty in recruiting twenty-five men for the expedition to Delagoa Bay.

Their ages ranged from fifteen to sixty, and they were as representative a bunch of schemers, scallywags and footloose adventurers as one would expect to find in those circumstances.

To most of them, at the outset, Tom and Will were no more than mascots or butts for their good or bad humour, although a man's full share of work was expected of them. But they had their champions in Kangaroo Joe and a herculean Highlander from Skye named Macpherson, who took the young Irishman Will Scully into his protection when a powerful bully named Collins began to give Will a rough time on their first day out.

The thrashing Macpherson gave Collins established the fact once and for all that anyone ill-treating young Scully would have Macpherson to reckon with.

Among the party were the Bos'n, Brother Bill, Big Macpherson, Artful Joe, Collins, Gilbert and others whom Major MacDonald had summed up with a very shrewd eye and accepted for his own good reasons. There had been not a little argument among those who were rejected, which the Major had firmly stamped out right away.

'Just get this straight,' he told them. 'I'm not choosing you men because you're special buddies, nor yet for the beer barrels your legs have to support. I know stamina when I see it. And I know the kind of guy who'll see this thing through—on his hands and knees if need be, but without any whining. All right. No more arguing. I've got my twenty-five men and I'm satisfied with my choice. But I thank you others who came forward on behalf of the President and the Transvaal Republic.'

'Men, you call 'em? Some's not yet weaned!' one fellow shouted scornfully.

'Get off the bottle yerself, Whisky Willie, before you start

talkin' about whose food comes out of a bottle!' Kangaroo Joe had bellowed back.

He was in great form because his name had headed the list of recruits. It meant far more to him than if he had received a gold medal. In that mood only a fool would cross him.

In a matter of days they were on their way, cheered by friends and the disgruntled alike, for everyone knew that they faced a tough task. And the mountains echoed back the cheering.

The convoy included eight wagons and sixteen spans of oxen—two-hundred of the best beasts money could buy, although when the tsetse fly stung the strong fell along with the weak, and more than half of those oxen were indeed to die before the mission had ended.

The nightmare journey really began with the descent over the Drakensberg escarpment at Kowyn's Pass, a three-thousand-foot track that had been created with dynamite, crow-bar and axe over the past few months at the Government's expense.

How rightly the range had been named by the early Voortrekkers, 'Dragon's Mountain', for it posed the greatest test of nerve, strength and skill to those who would conquer it and press on.

Down, down they edged their way, wagon after wagon, the men straining to keep the oxen on the precipitous track and to hold back the wagons with chains and riems to prevent them from overturning or smashing into the inspanned beasts.

Down into the mysterious haze-shrouded Lowveld with only the insignificant Lebombo Range in the distance to break the smooth flow of the fly and fever country to the coast, 178 miles away.

In the foothills, close to Ship Mountain, Major MacDonald decided to establish a depot against their return. Eight spans of oxen were left there in the care of several men.

From then on the convoy would be travelling over plains infested by the dreaded tsetse fly. Their plan was to press on with all speed, gambling on the six weeks' lag before oxen succumbed after having been stung.

The country teemed with wild life of all kinds, and the plains were sparsely timbered and densely covered with thick, wiry grass through which the wagons moved as though through deep amber waters.

At the end of each day the party would encamp, drawing the wagons into a double line. Then the animals would be grazed and watered while the men gathered huge quantities of fire-wood, which was plentiful. Before nightfall the oxen would be secured to the staked-down trek-chains, and the ring of six large fires would be kept burning all night, with relays of four men always on guard to tend the fires and keep the ever-present lions at bay.

The trail they followed had rightly been called The Death Trail. For it had first been beaten by the shuffling feet of ranks of slaves under the whips of Arab raiders. Gold and ivory traders had also passed that way in the distant past, as the ancient diggings on the Highveld proved. And, since the recent rediscovery of alluvial gold in the Eastern Transvaal, other men had tramped up from Delagoa Bay. The bones of many signposted the terrible route.

They crossed the wide, clear waters of the Crocodile and Komati Rivers without incident, although many crocodiles basked on the banks and on the rocks between which the waters eddied.

In the groves of magnificent trees that grew to the water's edge buffalo, giraffe, water buck, and wild life of many kinds were seen.

Only the elephants had apparently learned to keep at a safe distance from men, for they were never actually seen. Tom, who was becoming increasingly interested in wild life and its ways, occasionally spotted the spoor of elephants and was quick to tune in to their trumpeting in the distance as the huge beasts crashed through the trees.

It was after they had crossed the Komati and were approaching the Lebombo Range that the expedition chanced upon a typical bushveld tragedy.

Early one morning they saw a tent-wagon standing in a thickly wooded hollow. Fever trees draped and encrusted with bright yellow lichen surrounded it, under which lay the putrefying carcases of several oxen.

Major MacDonald halted the convoy and went to investigate. Under the wagon he found four men who were obviously dying of fever, and were raving in delirium. There were no signs of food or water in the vicinity, and the men were at once given what help was possible. That they were French was obvious from their raving. Small mounds in the vicinity of the wagon proved to be human graves. Sand had simply been heaped over the bodies.

The men were being carried to one of the wagons when a gigantic bearded man emerged from the bush and staggered towards them. He carried a small demijohn in each hand.

It was Will Scully who recognized the man as being Isadore Alexandre, a Frenchman he had known on the Kimberley diamond fields.

When he had been given food and drink this man explained how tragedy had overtaken his expedition, originally eight strong, which had started out from Lydenburg six weeks previously, bent on reaching Delagoa Bay.

All the oxen had succumbed more quickly than usual to the sting of the tsetse fly, and his companions had gone down with fever.

'Three of my men have died,' he said. 'I couldn't dig graves. That was the best I could do for them. It seemed we were all doomed until you came along to save us. Lions have given us no rest at night, and I have only a few cartridges left. You have come just in time, my friends. Only last night a lion carried off my dog from beside me at the fire. They knew that time was running out for us, and every night they became bolder.' He shuddered and passed a hand across his eyes as though he would wipe away the nightmare memories.

'Look at the ground all round the wagon, Tom,' Will said. 'There's not a hand's breadth anywhere near the camp that's not marked by lions' spoor.'

The nearest water was ten miles away, and to this spring Alexandre had trudged every day with his two demijohns to fetch water for his fever-stricken friends.

As the convoy moved on its way Tom thought the wagon looked like a stranded ship. He knew he would always remember it when he thought of the Lowveld.

The empty wagons were light and the oxen in good condition, so that the journey to the port was made in record time as the Major had planned.

They all realized that the homeward journey would be a very different experience, and so, when Delagoa Bay came in sight, the men began to go wild in anticipation of the good time they intended to have 'while the going was good'.

The little town lay between the bay and a crescent-shaped swamp which was crossed by several causeways. Between the swamp and the houses stood a fortified wall, and the town was dominated by a fortress of very evil reputation.

For several miles along the road approaching Delagoa Bay the trees were loaded with children who had swarmed out to gape at the large convoy, rumours of which reached the town by Native runners. Most of the people of the town were Banyans, with Portuguese in all posts of authority.

'Hell's going to break loose here tonight, Tom,' Will said from his greater experience. 'If we stick close together it will be all right, and it could be fun.'

The only hotel was a large, comfortable house kept by a Portuguese named Fernandez and his English wife. And this MacDonald's men immediately took over. Shops were looted, and in no time the town was in a state of siege with the inhabitants hiding behind barred doors, and even the police shutting themselves away in the safety of the prison dungeons.

It was Big Macpherson who discovered the obsolete fire-brigade uniforms in one of the raided shops. These had massive burnished metal guards to cover chest and back, and theatrical helmets, and the men pounced on them when Big Mac doled them out.

Even Kangaroo Joe was persuaded to don a helmet in place of his beloved hat, which he was careful to fold up and stuff into his shirt for safe keeping.

Dressed in these comic-opera uniforms MacDonald's men prepared to paint the town red.

Conditions in the hotel became riotous and Macpherson took Tom and Will in tow.

'Let's away an' have a wee bit of a lark on our own, lads,' he suggested, his booming voice rough with its Scots twang. 'It's a grand opportunity with the police safely locked away and all.'

Big Mac made straight for the Governor's residence, signalling for silence as they approached the impressive building with its walled grounds, and gates that were permanently open on rusted hinges.

Two sentries paced the footpath between the gates and the

archway leading to an inner courtyard. Over this archway hung a fine pair of kudu horns, and tropical trees, palms and shrubs cast deep shadows across the path.

No sooner had the sentries wheeled and turned their backs on the gates than the three revellers slipped into the grounds. Big Mac led the way over the shadowed lawn, reaching the archway after the sentries had about turned for their march back to the gates.

Suddenly, everything seemed to happen at once. A sharp order stopped the three in their tracks, and they turned to find their path of retreat blocked by the two sentries with fixed bayonets, which they would certainly not have hesitated to use.

Quick as thought Big Mac reached up and tore the kudu horns from the wall. Holding the skull to his chest he charged the stupified sentries, uttering terrible Highland war cries. He was enough to strike terror into bigger and braver men by far than the two diminutive Portuguese, and it was no wonder they dropped their guns and ran.

Big Mac caught one sentry before he reached the gates, but the other tore down the street screaming blue murder.

'I've no intention of harming you, wee mon,' Macpherson declared, picking the sentry up and cramming him into the sentry-box which he then overturned, trapping the man underneath.

Lights were appearing in many of the windows of the great house, and there were loud voices and commands.

'We'll no' be taking the Governor's firearms. He'll maybe need them before the night's through,' Macpherson said blandly.

He and Will each grabbed a bayoneted rifle from the footpath and stuck them in a flower-bed.

Then they were off, with the sound of gunfire from the house marking their retreat.

It was a safe bet that Will and Tom were the only members of Major MacDonald's expedition to face the next day without a splitting headache.

Delagoa Bay seemed like a town of the dead. Not a soul appeared. All shops were shut. The soldiers were barricaded up in the fort with the canon trained on the streets.

'We've surely cooked our goose, Will,' Tom said, as they stood on the wide veranda of the hotel looking out across the silent town to where the ship was anchored. 'They'll never let us have the guns and ammunition we've come all this way for, now.'

Will laughed.

'Don't you believe it! They'll be glad to see the last of us. And they know very well that we won't leave without our load—half of it, anyway. Seems we're going to have to make two trips.'

He was right. Everything was done to ensure that the port was rid of MacDonald and his men as quickly as possible, even though they had to do all the work of offloading themselves. The harbour workers had mysteriously disappeared.

The wagons were stacked with five-pound bags of gunpowder contained in one-hundred pound kegs loosely knocked together and hooped with saplings. There was also a canon with a copper plate impressively inscribed *Le Général Schuter*, which had to be drawn by eight oxen.

About five days' trek from the port they came to the dreaded Mattol Marsh, which was a quagmire several hundred yards across.

On their forward journey they had felled trees and laid a corduroy road across it, which the empty wagons had crossed without mishap. But now the improvised road gave way under the weight of the wagons and there was nothing for it but to shoulder every keg through the mud, taking great care that they remained dry. It was gruelling work. The wagons had then to be dismantled and carried across piecemeal.

No men could have been more sober than the weary chaps who eventually reassembled and loaded the wagons, and then moved on.

Nor was that the only swamp that had to be crossed in this laborious and painful way. Soon, from much handling, the barrels began to break up, and the men had to deal with the bags. Then these in turn gave way, and loose gunpowder permeated everything. The men tasted it in their food and tea and shook it from their kits when they unrolled them at night. Their eyes were bloodshot, their lips cracked with it.

'NO SMOKING NEAR THE WAGONS!' Major MacDonald bellowed time and again, until he realized that warnings were useless. The men refused to give up smoking, and were apparently past caring if they were indeed blown up.

'Just look at them!' Tom exclaimed one day when they were all taking a much needed rest. 'Actually lying there on the ground under that wagon for shade, and every man jack of them smoking!' He and Will watched the trickles of grey powder as it fell among the smokers, and marvelled that they were not all blown sky high.

Death took one life and came perilously close to all of them when a grass fire swept towards the convoy one day. A stiff wind whipped it on and it seemed that nothing but a miracle could save their highly explosive cargo from blasting them all to eternity.

They were outspanned at the Komati Drift, and the men were powerless to do anything but stand and watch the pall of smoke and leaping flames as they raced their way.

Major MacDonald gave the order that, when the fire reached a certain point, they were to abandon their wagons to their fate and take to the river with all haste. As the river teemed with crocodiles it could well have been no more than a choice between two violent deaths.

'If it's to be the river, kick up all hell,' Kangaroo Joe told Tom. 'If we rush it, raising as much row as we can, there's just a hope we may scare the crocs off—us and the fire together. But—hey, look at the wind, boys, look at the wind!' he suddenly shouted.

It was uncanny to watch the impossible happening before their eyes. For that is just what every man believed it to be.

Suddenly, the wind had died. One moment it had been thrusting the flames high in the air and rushing the fire forward; the next—it had blown itself out.

'Your shirts! Rush it before the wind gets up again. Now we've a chance to beat it out!' Major MacDonald bellowed, stripping off his own shirt and tearing into action.

The wagonloads of gunpowder and the crocodile-infested river were spurs enough, and the men leapt forward to meet the fire all along its line of approach.

The crackle of the flames and shouts of the men as each of them beat away at the fire must have drowned the cries of Sandy McWilliams. If indeed he had time to cry out.

It was only later that they found his body, when the fire had been subdued and Major MacDonald was directing the wagons across the Drift, anxious lest another wind should spring up, another smouldering spark be fanned to life. They could hardly expect a second miracle to save them.

Two wagons had already crossed the river. The third was about to follow.

'Where's McWilliams?' the Major asked sharply. 'I haven't seen him since the fire.' He cupped his hands to his mouth and shouted ahead, 'Hey, there! Is McWilliams with you? McWilliams—where is he?'

They found his body, and they buried him on the spot. It seemed he must have been blinded by the smoke and had probably stumbled over something—a hole, perhaps, or the root of a tree—and struck his head on a boulder. Then the fire was upon him.

'There's a good chance that he didn't know anything about it,' Major MacDonald told the subdued men gathered round their comrade's grave. 'Let's thank our stars he was the only one.'

Because the men were even more anxious to press on than before, now they occasionally trekked by moonlight.

On one such night Kangaroo Joe, Will and Tom had walked ahead of the leading wagon. It was a night full of the strange bushveld magic that, once experienced, has called men back from the ends of the earth.

Silver moonlight flooded the vast plains, dwarfing trees and bushes by comparison with the limitless canopy of the sheltering sky. The stars swung low, pulsing, alive. 'Like a host of angels,' Will thought. The night wind, trailing through the tall, brittle grass, made soft sweet sounds as though fingers stroked the strings of harps. He was, as so often, in a world of his own, bewitched, and full of inner word-music and imagery.

Kangaroo Joe and Tom were talking in the comfortable, intimate way of close friends, about all manner of things.

Suddenly the big man froze in his tracks.

'Sh-h!' he whispered. It was hardly louder than a sigh.

There, not five yards away, were a lion and lioness, crouched flat in the roadway. Waiting. Watching them with steady amber eyes and no movement.

The same thought struck the three men simultaneously. They were unarmed. They had left the convoy some way behind.

Tom and Will fused their attention on Kangaroo Joe. Very slowly, hardly seeming to move, they stepped backwards.

Kangaroo's eyes never flickered from the lions'. Their tawny colouring blended perfectly with track and grass.

For about fifty yards they moved back in slow motion, hardly daring to breathe. It seemed a separate lifetime—endless and tense.

Then—'RUN!' whispered Kangaroo Joe. And they turned and sprinted for their lives, not slackening their pace until they met the first wagon.

By the time the convoy reached their depot at Ship Mountain several of the oxen were showing the first signs of sickness.

'It's about-turn with all speed,' Major MacDonald told his men. 'As soon as we've buried these loads in dry sand here, the wagons must go back to Delagoa for the rest of the cargo. Six of you men will remain here in charge. We'll take fresh oxen and hit out first thing tomorrow morning. And no skylarking at the port this time, either!'

'As though we ever did!' muttered Big Mac.

To their unashamed relief Tom and Will were among those chosen to remain behind. So were Kangaroo Joe and three other men. Big Macpherson had to make the double trip. He preferred it that way.

'I canna abide the stink of dying cattle,' he said cryptically.

And Tom and Will were soon to share his feelings. Almost at once the doomed cattle began to die. As they showed signs of collapse they were driven to a spot about a mile from the camp, where they died quickly.

The nights were made hideous by the devil's chorus of hyenas, jackals and lions, as they fell upon the dead beasts.

The only water for miles around was within ten yards of the tents, which had been erected near a clump of tall trees. And here the lions used to drink at night, padding round and round the camp despite the fires and the occasional shots fired into the air to scare them off.

It was an uneasy watch the men kept.

As days stretched into weeks the waiting seemed unbearable at times. The men's gloom arose not only from their inaction, but from the steady death toll among the stricken oxen, and the slight bouts of fever most of the men suffered, which caused their temperatures to rise and fall sharply, and resulted in depression.

One dark night something happened that was to haunt Tom and Will for the rest of their lives. The fact that no logical explanation was ever found to account for it, added to the deep impression it made on them.

Men do not readily believe in ghosts.

A heavy blanket of haze covered the plains, completely obscuring the sky, so that there was not even the light and comfort of the stars on that moonless night.

Tom was stoking the fires and feeling alone as never before, when his ear caught the sound of a distant cry—'Hull—oo. Hul—loo.' Although it was far off, it was clear, and was coming nearer.

'Kangaroo! Will! Listen—there's a man calling out there!' Tom roused the sleeping men, thankful that he was, in fact, not alone.

'It's a man all right. Lost, by the sound of him, poor devil. Come on, heap wood on the fire! Fetch your guns—we'll direct him this way by shots and firelight.'

Nearer and nearer came the voice. Tom kept the fire blazing high with Will's help. Guns were fired into the air at frequent intervals, and the men waved firebrands and shouted answering hulloes.

No one doubted that it was a human voice. It came within perhaps three-hundred yards of the camp, uttering its heart-rending cry at intervals. And then—it began to grow fainter. Whoever —*whatever*—it was slowly passed on, the cries becoming no more than a distant echo of sound. Then it was gone.

'My God!' Kangaroo Joe whispered.

The six men stood as though frozen, staring at each other in the small circle of firelight.

It was Will Scully who broke the silence. 'I'd heard that they come back on nights like this. But I never thought—' His throat was dry.

'A billycan of tea—and make it strong, Tom!' Kangaroo Joe suddenly shouted. 'Ghosts! Why, if the ghosts of all the chaps who've died on this bloomin' trail was to come back to haunt the livin'—a fine old chorus that'd be. Ferget it, boys. We'll be laughin' about it come morning.'

But no one did laugh. Nor could any of them be persuaded that it had been other than the voice of a man—a human voice calling in the wilderness. Alive—or dead!

*

And then one day the convoy came in sight, a faint plume of dust in the far distance, first sighted by Tom from the topmost branches of one of the trees that sheltered the camp.

Thankfully the men threw themselves into feverish activity, uncovering the buried gunpowder, preparing food for the approaching party.

Kangaroo Joe voiced the feelings of them all when he said with grim satisfaction:

'We'll soon be outta here now, boys. An' it can't be too soon fer me!'

Unable to bear the pace of an ox, he loped off to meet the crawling convoy, waving his red shirt, tied to a stick, in welcome.

There was a dreamlike quality about the rest of the journey and the drag up over the escarpment. Everyone was too tired to think clearly, too exhausted by the long ordeal to do more than obey orders with what strength they could muster.

The remaining oxen were so weak that the men had frequently to unload and literally put their shoulders to the wheel. It was also necessary to manhandle the cargo up the precipitous trail. In their exhausted state the ordeal tested their endurance to the limit. Yet no man complained. Major MacDonald had known how to choose his men.

Not until they reached Lydenburg was their mission complete. The precious cargo was handed to the waiting authorities who would transport it to Pretoria, and the men were warmly thanked and paid off.

Tom McLachlan had a mule wagon at Lydenburg to take MacDonald and his men back to Pilgrim's Rest, where a great welcome awaited them.

They had set out early in June. It was now September. But Tom thought how true it was that some experiences could not be measured in time. He knew that he had changed in many ways during the past three months. He was tougher and more responsible. He had borne his fair share of the hardships and dangers. And he had come through. In the process Africa had forged him into a man. He had no regrets. No regrets whatever.

19

Tom Stakes His Claim

Samantha and Chris, with Nugget loping along at heel, had ridden up to the top of the Divide when news came that MacDonald's party could be expected in Pilgrim's Rest that afternoon.

Tom was the first to see the riders silhouetted against the skyline, and his throat felt tight. This time he had remembered Sam's birthday. He was sixteen that day—as she would be on the morrow.

Characteristically, she raced down the trail to meet the mule-wagon, her hair streaming in the wind.

Chris followed, thankful that Samantha rode so sure-footed a horse on that dangerously steep track, but anxious for all that. The chestnut mare had been his birthday present to Sam, and she had named it Diamond.

'If only my first dear horse had been salted, like this one,' she had said. 'Oh, Chris, there couldn't have been a more wonderful gift!' And she had kissed him, lightly, for the first time since the old Pretoria times when a kiss had held no more meaning than a hand clasp or a brotherly hug.

Everyone in the valley turned out to give the men the welcome they had earned. Then the pubs filled up, and, until the next morning, the mud was allowed to settle in the Blyde and the creeks while the men talked and drank, and went on talking far into the night.

Kangaroo Joe forgot his old aversion to eating under a roof and took his place at the table with the family, to which he now felt he belonged. Will Scully and Chris were also there.

Although Kangaroo Joe wore a new red flannel shirt to honour the occasion, his battered hat was firmly set on his head. But nobody seemed to notice it. Indeed, to the most of them, it had long ceased to be a hat. It had become part and parcel of the man himself.

As the oldest member of the expedition he felt justly proud of his recent performance. He'd stood the gruelling pace with the best of them, and only he knew what that had cost him at times.

'Are you satisfied now, Kangaroo Joe?' Samantha asked from down the table. 'Will you be able to settle down again and forget there's a world beyond this valley?'

'Never on yer sweet life, Sammy. That little walk jest reminded me, that's all. Reminded me of all the other valleys waitin' to be found. All the other gold that's waitin' to be turned up by my shovel and pan. Matter of fact I'll be hittin' out soon. A few matters to be fixed up here—then I'm off.'

'Where to now?' Tom asked, closely watching his friend.

'Waal, I'll tell you. But not a word to no one mind. It's secret. Fact is I met a chum who brought a message from an old buddy of mine. Got it before we lit out fer Delagoa, but I reckoned it could wait till we got back. This buddy—Rollingstone Charlie by name—'

'*Rollingstone Charlie!*' Tom and Chris exclaimed in chorus.

'Ah, yer know him? Good chap, old Rollingstone. We've fossicked together in California, Australia, New Zealand—'

'I've often wondered what became of him,' Tom said. 'Chris and I met him when we were hunting. He was making for Mac Mac then. What happened to him on the way?'

'He found this here place I'm tellin' yer about. No place names mentioned, y'understand. Jest the general direction. I guess I know where it is. Old Rollingstone an' me can smell each other out at a coupla hundred miles, come to that.'

'But if it's gold you want—' Andrew Howes put in.

'Not the *found* stuff. What good's that to a man? I'm arranging to leave all I've found here with the bank man. It's fer you, Tom, if you want it—or if I snuff out.'

'Kangaroo Joe!' There was pain in Tom's eyes.

'Oh, come off it. I'll live to a hundred or more shouldn't wonder.' The big man chuckled. 'But I guess I'm jest an old fossicker. Always was. Always will be. I'll be off to join Rollingstone Charlie. But I'll be back, buddy. Bet yer last dollar I'll be back. Yer stuck with me, I guess.'

'It would be terrible if we weren't,' Polly Howes said with

feeling. 'You're part of the family, now and always, Kangaroo Joe.'

'Thank you, ma'am. That's the way I feel. But I got to come and go as fancy takes me.'

'We understand,' Tom told him.'Just as long as you continue to come as well as go.'

'By the way, that reminds me,' Will said. 'What's happened to Richard Somers? I meant to ask you before we went off, and he's crossed my mind several times lately. Anyone know?'

Samantha kept her eyes on her plate, and her mother answered.

'Oh, didn't you know, Will?' she said casually. 'Richard went back to England. He'd found all the wealth he needed to get his family out of the trouble they were in, which was why he came here in the first place. We've heard from him since, but I don't think he'll come back. His roots are too deeply planted in the Old Country. He's not the type who can be happily transplanted.'

'Sam received a letter from him only the other day, didn't you, dear?'

The look Samantha gave her father told Tom all he needed to know.

'Bad luck for him,' he said, catching her eye, and smiling. 'Sam's such a rotten correspondent, I mean. Aren't you, Sam?'

'The world's worst,' she agreed shortly.

She was wearing the coral necklace Tom had brought her from Delagoa Bay. It matched her flushed cheeks.

'So much has been happening while you've been away, Tom,' Polly Howes said when the meal was over and they were all sitting round the fire. 'You heard about your claim, Will?'

Will Scully smiled.

'Imagine that chum who took my claim over actually lifting £2,000 from the very spot where my bed had been!'

'The bottom legs were actually touching the gold,' Samantha said. 'It was too bad, Will!'

'Too bad? He's welcome to it. If he's found all that gold, and much more, on my old claim, think what there must be on other parts of Theta. I'm going to stake a new claim there first thing in the morning. This time I'm sure to strike it lucky!'

'Good luck to you, chum!' Tom said. 'But I sometimes wonder

if it's gold you're really after and not, well, stars and ocean beds and eagles and things.'

'It's gold all right,' Will declared, but his eyes belied it. Their fire was not the fanatical flame of the gold-enchanted. It was reflected from deep within.

'And you, Tom?' his uncle asked. 'Do you still want to stake a claim in this country? And what do you want to do? You've had time to think, just as we have.'

'I know very well what I want to do, Uncle Andrew. But I don't know how it will affect your plans.'

'Fire away.'

'Well, our claims are about worked out here, aren't they?'

'We could stake others, if that's what you want.'

Tom shook his head.

'No, it isn't. May I tell you my plans—on the understanding, of course, that they fit in with all of yours?'

'Of course.'

'I'm a South African. And I don't love England any less because of it. But this is where I feel I belong.' He threw a log onto the fire, then went on steadily: 'We've been very lucky, haven't we? I mean, we've found enough gold to see all of us through anything we may want to do. I'm right, aren't I?'

'Perfectly true. Carry on.'

'Well, I know I could improve my education. Go to college and all that. But I don't want to. I feel I don't need to—for the work I'm going to do. What I want and need is practical experience and the right kind of training—here in South Africa. I'm through with digging for gold. It was a grand experience, but I've had enough of it. I didn't really know what I wanted to

do—what I was looking for—until I began thinking down in the Lowveld. I've thought a lot—and I know now all right.'

Tom hesitated, then went on.

'I want to study wild life, Uncle Andrew. It seems to me it's about time we started to think about protecting it, and stopped this wholesale killing that's been going on. Seeing the way the elephants have been practically wiped out on the Highveld here—the way they've learned to hide from us men with guns on the Lowveld. The way most hunters just shoot game down—buck, giraffe, quagga, anything that provides them with an interesting target—well, it makes me sick! Shoot for the pot, yes. They kill to eat too. But just to destroy them—?'

'Oh, Tom, I knew you'd feel like that,' Samantha cried. 'Shooting for the fun of it is beastly.'

Chris leant forward.

'You know why I hunt, Tom,' he said earnestly. 'I've explained that to you, haven't I? I'm a farmer, not a hunter by choice. It won't be long now before it will be possible to farm full time. To plant those forests and orchards and—'

'Yes, I know how it is with you, Chris. Of course I understand it,' Tom assured him. 'You're a farmer. But I'm not interested in growing things. It's the wild life that's got me. Major MacDonald was telling me about a scheme that's taking shape in Pretoria to set aside enormous tracts of land for game reserves, and to train men to patrol them. That's the work I want to do. To study wild-life conservation. But how does it fit in with your plans, Uncle Andrew?'

Andrew Howes reached across and took his wife's hand in his.

'We've made our plans too, Tom. And they do fit in perfectly with yours, since that's the way you want it. You see, your aunt and I are townsfolk. My chosen profession—the work I'm good at—fits me for the city rather than the wilds. And it's work I enjoy. You know that your aunt will never really be a country woman. She's adapted herself to these conditions and made this great experience possible for all of us, but—'

His wife cut in.

'Tom, let me be honest with you, as I've been with your uncle and Samantha—and with myself. I rejected this country from the moment I stepped off the boat. I was appalled at the primitive

conditions, the lack of comforts and the things I'd always loved about my gay life in London.'

Polly Howes was smiling, and Tom thought how lovely she was—just as he had always known her in England.

'I deliberately shut my eyes and my heart to—to just everything about this country,' she went on. 'Why, do you know, I can't even remember clearly what D'Urban and Pietermaritzburg are like! Well, while you were away on the expedition, your uncle asked me if I wanted to go back to London now that we have the money, and it would be possible for us to do so. But I find I don't want to go, Tom. I really don't. What I want to do—what we're going to do—is this. We're going back to the beginning of our South African experience. We're going to start again. Your uncle, Samantha and I are going down to D'Urban—with my eyes and heart wide open this time! Your uncle will do his kind of work there. I'll be able to make a real home for us. And Samantha should finish her sadly neglected education—'

'Oh, Mama!' Samantha cried.

'I said you *should* finish your education, darling. But, like Tom, I think you've experienced too much in the past year to return to the classroom. You don't have to tell your father and me that this is your life, Samantha. It's as though you were born to it.'

She looked from her daughter to the young man beside her, including Christian le Roux in her smile.

'I don't think it will be long before you return here, Samantha—with our blessing,' she added.

'And what will become of your house here in Pilgrim's Rest?' Will asked, to draw attention away from Sam and Chris, who were obviously too absorbed in each other to wish for attention to be focused on them.

'This house? Oh, we'll keep it, Will. We couldn't bear to part with it. It will always be a holiday home, a second home, for any of us to come back to. Friends can also use it. But we'll never part with it. How could we, with all the memories it holds for us all?'

They drank a toast to each other that night, and the road each had chosen to follow. Roads that would lead far and wide—and yet were to remain as one road to the end.

Last Word

This book is about real people and true events. The only names you won't find in the pages of South African history are those of Tom Maxwell, Samantha and her parents, Kangaroo Joe and Christian le Roux. And yet even they are real people—if composite. They came to life for me during the eighteen years that I've spent tracking down and listening to Old Timers from the Roaring Seventies and their descendants, studying many books and old publications, and masses of unpublished diaries, scrapbooks, letters and photographs, as well as visiting the places where the action in this book took place.

The village of Pilgrim's Rest has recently been proclaimed a National Monument. And Mac Mac is again much as it was before the frenzy of the Gold Rush so roughly disturbed it.

One of the great moments of my life was when Meg Howes, her daughter, Peta Cramb, who was born in Pilgrim's Rest, and I discovered and stood on the foundations of Herbert Rhodes's 'Spotted Dog', half hidden by pine needles and bracken. A forest of pines now covers the hill on the first step of which Rhodes built his notorious pub, but it is still a warren of shallow old claims, with many of the wooden props still standing. And ghosts galore!

Looking out across the crescent valley, as Rhodes and McLachlan, MacDonald and Scully, and all those other Old Timers must have done so often, we saw the gentle curves of the meandering river and where it plunged over the escarpment at Mac Mac Falls—forever broken into twin curtains of water by the charge of dynamite laid by that nameless, gold-mad digger, so long ago. The music of the Falls is the only sound in the sleeping valley these days, other than birdsong, the wind in the pines, and the occasional car on the wide macadamized road that has replaced the original track.

Pilgrim's Rest is still a one-street hamlet, now smothered in the greenery of trees, so that Pilgrim's Creek, which again flows sweetly over its bed of rocks and gold-glittering sand, is for ever shaded and mostly hidden.

Theta Hill still wears an innocent mantle of grass and wild flowers, and a few healed scars show where Will Scully and his fellow diggers staked their claims and dug shallow workings. Yet under that mantle the hill is honeycombed with tunnels, and as active as any anthill. It is nearly one hundred years since the day Will picked up the 'feather' nugget on what has proved to be the richest single deposit of gold in the world, yet gold is still being taken from Theta by the Transvaal Gold Mining Estates, who long ago bought up the mining rights.

Will Scully was right in believing that the gold found in Pilgrim's Creek had been washed down from this hill of gold over the ages. But he never 'struck it rich' himself in a material sense. Instead, he became a magistrate and renowned poet and author, and so contributed his own immortal wealth to the land he loved and adopted.

In a drawer of my desk is the red and gold tin marked 'Blakey', which once held metal boot tips and is still full of the rubies and garnets—his 'fiery stones'—which Will Scully gathered and cherished for their beauty. It was placed in my keeping by my dear friend and Will Scully's youngest daughter, Betty Gray, who is a poet and visionary, dedicated to Life and attuned to the voices of Nature, even as he was.

Tom Maxwell may have been a composite character who grew for me out of much study and experience. But I know what his future held for all that. He was to become one of the great pioneer wild life Conservationists to whom we owe so much here in Southern Africa.

FAY GOLDIE

Glossary

BAAS	Master (frequently used as a form of address).
BRAAIVLEIS	Grilling meat over open fire or barbecue.
BOEREWORS	Sausage.
KOPPIE	Small hill.
LAAGER	Camp; encampment, especially in circle of wagons.
MAGTIG	Exclamation of surprise or annoyance. (Afrikaans.)
MENEER	Mister (frequently used as a form of address). (Afrikaans.)
MEVROU	Madam, Mrs. (usual form of address). (Afrikaans.)
RIEM	Thong.
SJAMBOK	Whip made of rhino hide or other thick hide.
STOEP	Veranda, covered or uncovered.
VELSKOEN	Shoes made of rough leather.
VLEI	Hollow in which water collects during rainy season.
VOORLOOP	Leading a span of oxen.
VOORTREKKER	Pioneer. Afrikaners who ventured into the interior of Southern Africa in search of independence.